THE ALIEN'S MATE

Earthly Mates

Book 1

ANNABELLE MARIN

Published by Blushing Books
An Imprint of
ABCD Graphics and Design, Inc.
A Virginia Corporation
977 Seminole Trail #233
Charlottesville, VA 22901

The Alien's Mate
Annabelle Marin

EBook ISBN: 978-1-63954-470-7
Print ISBN: 978-1-63954-471-4

Chapter 1

"ALICE! ALICE! HALT, PLEASE."

Alice Andrews let out a loud sigh as she forced her sneaker-covered feet to stop when in reality she wanted to run in the opposite direction, even though the twenty-two-year-old was not exactly known for her athletic ability.

Even *if* she had been some hot shot athlete on a scholarship, she doubted her short legs could outrun him. The *him* Alice was currently talking about and the persistent thorn in her side was Kyvan. No last name, just Kyvan.

In the few short conversations she'd had with him, he had mentioned he was a foreign exchange student who had somehow landed his hot ass in her tiny private liberal arts college in remote Vermont.

They had meet two weeks ago in passing, when he had accidentally bumped into her when she had been nose deep into her planner trying to figure out how many more weeks until her college graduation. Since then, he hadn't left her alone even though Alice considered herself a pretty forgettable person who enjoyed her alone time.

Despite her cold shoulder, Kyvan was a pretty persistent

man from France or Germany or perhaps even Demark. He had never given her a straight answer when she inquired about it. All Alice knew was he had a thick accent, was stupid hot, and used old-fashioned words like "halt" and "versed." Once, Alice had even caught him poring through an old English dictionary from the 1970s.

Still, she couldn't simply dismiss him. For starters, the puppy dog eagerness he had for her had resulted in the jealousy of her roommates which had never happened before, and the larger reason being she didn't want to graduate college a virgin. Kyvan's golden retriever energy was a hell of a lot more welcoming than a surly TA or a stupid frat boy.

"You walk fast," Kyvan mentioned once he reached her in what seemed like three easy steps. "It is an excellent skill to have when potential danger arises."

Alice forced a smile on her face. Kyvan might be handsome, standing at an impressive six foot eight, with dark curly hair that reached his bulky shoulders, striking green eyes, and a chiseled six pack, but it didn't change the fact he was so goddamn weird. Maybe he had grown up in a weird cult before he packed his bags and headed to stalk her in Vermont.

Sure, he showered her with compliments and carried her belongings when they had class in the same building, but it didn't change the fact that the majority of their conversations these past two weeks had gone a little like this: "Would you say you are a relatively healthy young woman?" and "How are the birth rates in your family?" And, of course, she couldn't forget the best one, "Your wide hips are perfect for childbearing, has anyone told you?"

Not to mention, he always seemed to be watching her or close enough to ward off any other potential males who tried to chit chat with her. Being six foot eight and built like a Greek god, made it really hard to blend into the background.

Alice chuckled awkwardly. "Well, thankfully, there is no danger here." She moved her arms to motion to the large forest which surrounded the tiny college. "See, perfectly safe."

One of the reasons she had moved to Vermont for college after her single mom had passed away from cancer two weeks after her high school graduation was because she had wanted to get away from the city, the crowds, and the unnecessary noises. While others might have freaked out being so far away from "civilized society", Alice thrived in the peaceful nature.

"There is always danger, my little Alice." Kyvan's eyes flickered strangely, and for a second, they seemed to change from their deep green color. "You shouldn't dismiss it so easily, especially when it could be closer than you think."

"I'm not little." Alice waved away his warning. It was true she was five foot seven, taller than most other girls, but next to Kyvan, she might as well be an elf. She tugged on her long, black hair which she had neatly braided earlier. "Can I help you with anything, Kyvan?"

The serious expression left his face, to be replaced by a large grin. "Yes, I was hoping we could partake in each other's company tonight. I will bring sweets."

Alice snorted. He was making her seem like a dog who could be lured away with promises of cake and cookies. "Thank you, but I have a date tonight."

Daria Miller, her roommate, had set her up on a blind date with her cousin, Kevin, and the three of them were going to a party tonight hosted by Daria's boyfriend. She wasn't particularly excited about going, but Daria said she couldn't spend the rest of her senior year studying in her dorm room.

Kyvan's mood darkened as he narrowed his eyes at her. He suddenly leaned forward, gripping her wrist. It didn't hurt, but it was firm enough she wouldn't be able to shake him off. "A date? With another potential mate?"

"A mate? I'm not a bird. Ow, that hurts, Kyvan, let me go," Alice hissed. Kyvan loosened his iron grip but didn't let go. There was still a frown on his handsome face and she would be lying if she said it didn't make him look more handsome. "I'm single. I'm allowed to date, which I'm doing right now."

Kyvan pouted, still holding on to her as if she were a life preserver. "Alice, don't go. I'll be your mate, not another male. I'll take you on a date tonight and give you all the sweets you want."

"Thank you, but I have plans." She used the opportunity to slip her wrist out of his mean grip. He looked like he was about to place her over his shoulder and carry her like a caveman from a bad TV movie, but then his features relaxed.

"I see. I'll see you later, little Alice." He no longer looked angry. More like serene. Like he could see into the future and he was the winner while she played the part of the loser. She didn't know which was worse.

Alice chuckled as she jogged to the Communications building for her first class of her day. "I doubt it, Kyvan."

Later in the evening, close to midnight, Alice was drinking a lukewarm beer in Daria's boyfriend's home pretending to be interested in the conversation with her date of the evening, Kevin.

Her jaw was starting to hurt from fake smiling, but she didn't know how to politely tell Kevin the conversation bored her. He had been talking about his latest fishing trip for the past thirty minutes, and Alice was about to cry from boredom. She should have stayed home tonight,

Alice tugged on her short black dress and looked over Kevin's shoulder, hoping to catch Daria's attention to let her know she wanted to leave, but Daria was too busy making out with her boyfriend to even look in Alice's direction.

She let out an annoyed huff.

Kevin stopped talking about the best way to remove the eyeballs from a fish's carcass. "Are you okay?"

Alice forced a wobbly smile on her face. "Yes, I just need to go to the bathroom."

"Cool. I'll wait here for you. I have this great story about the time my dad and I went fishing in Montana. You'll laugh your ass off."

"Can't wait!"

Alice waited until Kevin was distracted to sneak out of the house, instead of heading to the restroom. The house was surrounded by drunk college kids, so it was easy to escape unnoticed.

Her heels clicked on the pavement as she walked a few houses down to call for an Uber. The last thing she wanted was to wait outside Daria's boyfriend's house and get caught by Kevin, trying to escape.

Once she had confirmed her ride, Alice waited impatiently for the car to show up as she shivered in her too-short dress. She was on her phone texting Daria a lame excuse indicating she wasn't feeling well when she was suddenly surrounded by bright white light.

At first, she thought it was her ride, but then the lights got bigger. Much too big to belong to a regular car. Alice let out a loud scream. The bright light was coming straight at her, blinding her.

Then, darkness.

Followed by silence.

The brunette wasn't sure how much time had passed when her blue eyes opened. Her head felt heavy, like she was underwater, her body half asleep, as if her muscles had stopped working.

Alice tried to sit up but found she couldn't. Her entire body was strapped to a cold, metal table, the kind used in morgues. She opened her mouth to scream, but only a whimper came out. It was as if her vocal chords had stopped functioning.

A breeze passed through her, causing her thighs to tighten and her pink nipples to pucker like tight little nubs in response. A wave of horror passed through her. She was naked.

Who had taken her clothes? Was it the same person who had taken her from the party? What were they going to do to her? Steal her organs? Cut her eyeballs out? She should have never listened to Daria and gone to the stupid party.

"Relax," a calm voice said as large gray hands palmed her cheeks as if trying to comfort her. "You're very nervous. Your heart rate is elevated, it's not good for your body."

Alice raised her face. At least the voice sounded kind. She immediately regretted the thought when she saw the scene in front of her. Three men were staring at her as if she were a rabbit at the petting zoo. Though she was using the term "men" loosely.

They were extremely tall, with deep gray skin and thick, pulsing veins surrounding their muscled bodies. Their hair was of different shades, but the majority of them wore it long. The one who had tried to calm her down seemed to be the oldest of the three, with snowy white hair. Their front teeth were sharp and pointy like a snake's, but the worst part was their eyes. They were the color of blood. Large and red, like they belonged to the devil himself.

They were monsters.

Some sort of devilish creatures.

She didn't know if they were worse than humans.

Frightened tears started pouring down her face as her

entire body trembled with fear. Her pink lips swelled by how hard she was biting them.

"Put her back to sleep, Orval," the creature with red hair ordered with disgust. "These human females are so sensitive. They're like children who cry at the smallest thing. How they have survived for centuries is still a wonder. I told the king we should have chosen another species, but he seemed to be soft on this one."

"It is because they bring better results," Orval mentioned as he pulled out a large needle. "Without human females, we would have died out a long time ago. It is best if you remember that. Do not criticize our king, for he knows what is best. Sleep, little one."

Alice felt a sharp prick on her thigh and then a burning sensation, as if her whole body had caught on fire. She wanted to scream, to plead for mercy. But almost as suddenly as the pain had come, it had also disappeared.

Once again, she was surrounded by darkness. This time, she welcomed it.

Anything was better than the creatures who had stood over her.

Chapter 2

THE AIR SMELLED LIKE RAIN.

Alice opened her blue eyes, jolted awake from her deep slumber. The one that had resulted in her nightmares, in which she had been surrounded, naked and bound, by three large, hellish creatures.

It took a moment for her vision to settle as it felt she had just exited a rollercoaster. Her muscles ached, especially her thigh where she had been poked with a needle. Her skin was so sensitive, she would probably bruise.

Alice raised her head and found her hands tied together with heavy iron ropes as she hung from the ceiling like a piece of meat. No wonder her body ached. Her feet were also bound tightly.

Surrounding her, were eighteen women between the ages of eighteen and thirty-five, equally naked. She had never seen so many bare breasts or round buttocks exposed in front of her. Their pubic hair had been removed, which meant Alice could see glimpses of their womanly charms hidden between their legs.

Some of the women were unconscious, while others, like

her, were starting to wake up like confused kittens. Confusion was replaced by fear as she tried to put the pieces together about what had happened. She had been waiting for a car to take her home when she had been surrounded by an obnoxious bright light, only to then be surrounded by strange looking gray creatures with red eyes and pointy fangs.

Now, here she was, tied up like a piece of meat for sale while the pink buds of her nipples hardened, thanks to the coldness of the room. The room was gray and held nothing of interest except for the several different branding irons heating in the nearby fireplace.

Alice flinched when she heard loud, masculine voices approaching, followed by stomping feet. She barely had time to react before the door was pushed open. She almost urinated on herself when she recognized the tall, gray men from earlier, though, this time, they were surrounded by twelve other men in various phases of excitement as they looked at the naked girls like they were their new toys.

All of the men, if Alice could call them that, were half naked and barefoot. The only thing covering their thick, muscled legs was a pair of short-like garments made of thick, black material. Alice could tell who the leader of their little group was right away. He was the tallest, with a bored expression, wearing a cape made out of red and black material across his wide shoulders.

He turned around and must have said something funny to his underlings because they all laughed. Alice didn't understand what they were saying, it all sounded like gibberish to her. She wiggled like a fish, but she might as well have been trying to drain the ocean.

She shut her blue eyes, hoping this was all a terrible dream caused by too many drinks at the party, but every time she opened her eyes, the current scene played before her like a walking nightmare. While the leader and the rest of his minions looked around at the remaining girls, one of the creatures approached her.

He pressed a long, thin hand across her cheek to caress it and the gesture was enough for Alice to burst into tears. Loud sobs exploded from her as her entire body shook with fear.

He stood back, confused, but his cold hand never left her face. He pursed his lips and said something to Alice she didn't understand. When she didn't stop crying, he frowned and reached his fingers to the back of her ear before pinching it roughly.

Alice yelped.

"They didn't turn your translator on. Now, do you understand me? My English is rather rough, it is better if we communicate this way. Easier for both of us."

The voice was smooth, assuring, and masculine, like a pilot announcing they would be arriving soon at their destination. It was also very familiar.

She stuck out her bottom lip, her trembling subsiding. "What are you?"

The creature still didn't answer as he peered at her curiously while he caressed her, his red eyes staring rather determinedly at her round, pale breasts.

It was clear this creature was not human, and they were not on Earth anymore if a translator had to be placed in her ear. Which meant the creature in front of her had to be some sort of alien or other unworldly creature. Alice always imagined aliens as short, green creatures with large heads and eyes, not gray men with demonic looks, built like bodybuilders.

The more the creature stared at her nude body, the more uncomfortable she became, until she started sobbing again. They were going to eat her, weren't they? Or experiment on her. She had seen this movie once, where—

The alien man frowned. "Don't cry, little Alice."

Little Alice?

No one called her that demeaning nickname other than Kyvan. How did this gray bastard know her name, anyhow?

The gray skin started disappearing, to be replaced by fair skin flushed by a healthy pink color. Familiar green eyes looked at her with concern as his lips pursed as if trying to find a way to comfort her,

His long pink tongue poked out of his lips to lick away the tears which had fallen across her cheeks. Alice was in too much shock to be weirded out. The gray villain had been replaced by dorky foreign exchange student Kyvan, but he was more intimidating than dorky right about now.

"Kyvan." Alice found her voice. "You're an alien or something?"

He nodded, almost apologetically. "Welcome to the planet, Krotev, little Alice. Your new home."

"What?"

Before she could protest any further, the man wearing the bulky red cape joined them. Unlike Kyvan, he stayed in his gray alien form. "This is the one you were telling me about, Kyvan?"

Kyvan nodded as he gave a respectful bow. "Yes, Your Majesty. This is my Alice. Alice, this is the King of Krotev, King Korrev." He gave her a sharp look which warned her to watch her tongue.

Alice didn't need to be warned, she was frightened of him already. Unlike Kyvan, who had a gentle expression, King Korrev looked at her as if she were dirt. He was also the only one of them wearing shoes, made of a sturdy brown material. He gave her the once over. "Fine. You may keep her. Consider her a reward for your excellent work in the battlefield."

"Thank you for your generosity."

"Excuse me, *keep* me?" she shrieked.

King Korrev raised an eyebrow in annoyance. He turned his back, ignoring her before giving his underling an I-hope-you-know-what-you're-doing expression. "Make sure you brand her, then take her back home to your quarters. The faster these hysterical females are paired off, the better."

"Of course."

"Hey!" Alice shouted at his turned back as she started wiggling around, knowing it was useless. "I am not done talking to you, how dare—"

Slap.

Her speech was cut off when she felt a sharp slap against her right buttock, leaving behind a pink handprint and aching feeling in its wake. Kyvan gripped her jaw firmly, but not enough to hurt her as he looked at her blue eyes. "Behave, little Alice. I'll explain everything, once I get you back to our quarters. Now, shut those pretty lips of yours, unless you want me to punish you before your branding."

Punish? What did he mean by that?

Kyvan spoke to another alien with bushy black hair, who was holding a branding iron which spelled out his name. He nodded once to the man before he pressed the hot branding iron against her plump left buttock.

The branding iron was pressed for ten seconds against her backside, searing her skin and carving Kyvan's name permanently on her ass.

Alice let out a loud scream as she felt the terrible burning pain on such a sensitive part of her body. Even when the hot iron was removed, her delicate skin throbbed as the alien's name flashed against the porcelain skin like a neon sign.

Loud sobs erupted from her as the sleepy-looking girls viewed her with alarm while Kyvan's buddies threw him dirty looks. Kyvan removed the bonds as he placed her over his shoulder like a sack of potatoes.

Alice was so focused on the raw pain she was feeling, she didn't care her bare ass was stuck in the air. Kyvan rubbed her lower back helplessly. "There, there, it's all over now, Alice. Nothing to cry about. It is to mark you, so everyone knows you're mine."

A hundred different swear words were at the tip of her tongue, but her humiliation was too much; she just focused on crying her eyes out as her new "owner" took her out of the strange little room.

Ten minutes later, Kyvan was unlocking a white door by pressing several numerical combinations, causing it to slide open. Once they were inside, he locked it once again and placed her down.

The burning pain on her ass from where his name had been engraved had been reduced to simple throbbing, which caused her tears to not fall with such ferocity. She craned her neck curiously to look at Kyvan's quarters.

It was large, with a tiny kitchen, a comfortable living room, bathroom, and from the bottom of the staircase, she could see three doors which led to different bedrooms. It looked like a regular apartment or condo from back on Earth, though much more minimalistic. Some of the things were a bit funny-looking, but overall, it seemed like a high-tech apartment.

Alice had been so busy looking at her new surroundings, she hardly noticed when Kyvan slipped a thick, light blue ribbon around her throat and closed the clasp with a loud click. The blue ribbon had a large bow at the back of her neck.

"What are you doing?" she squeaked as she grasped her throat.

"It's your new collar," the idiot said proudly. "It has a tracking device so I can see your every movement. Don't bother trying to remove it, only I have the key, and it's made out of resistible material."

Even though his voice was cheerful, Alice didn't miss the strong warning.

"Why a ribbon?" she demanded as she looked at herself in the mirror. She painted quite a pretty horrid picture— naked, with his name tattooed on her ass and a large bow around her neck. Almost looking like a present he was about to devour.

"When I was studying you on Earth, I saw humans decorate the collars they gave their pets. They looked rather adorable, and by placing the tracking on the collar instead of any part of your body, it will be less easy to remove. I convinced the other men to try it with their girls."

Alice flushed bright red as she fought the urge to punch him. "You thought it was adorable to dress me like a damn cat? I'm not an animal, Kyvan. I'm a person."

"Mate," he corrected quietly as he scooped her up in his arms and placed her on his lap. She squealed when her sore ass cheek touched his hard thigh which seemed to be made from concrete. "You're no longer simply an ordinary human, my little Alice. You are now my mate and will remain it until one of us dies."

Chapter 3

ALICE BIT HER TONGUE.

It wouldn't do anyone any good to lose her temper. She had to remind herself she was no longer dealing with Kyvan the dorky exchange student, she was dealing with a potentially dangerous alien who could quite easily hurt her and who seemed to blindly follow the king's orders, the one who had given her to him like a damn present.

"Start from the beginning," she forced herself to say. "Where are we, exactly? Not Earth, I assume."

"Not Earth," he confirmed, visibly relaxing as he started rubbing her taut stomach. His eyes visibly softened and this would be a romantic moment if he hadn't just kidnapped her. "We're close to Earth, though not close enough it can be seen by one of your flying trains."

"Spaceships," Alice murmured. Now it all made sense, how Kyvan was confused about the simplest things. He might have looked human, but he had never stepped foot on Earth until he had started chasing Alice down. "You mentioned this planet is called Krotev."

Kyvan nodded. "Yes, we're an all-male planet, ruled by King Korrev for decades."

"All male planet, how is it possible? Surely, you must have women who give birth to..." she blushed as she thought about another possibility. "Unless it works another way. No judgment here. After everything women have gone through, I think it's quite progressive men feel the pain of childbearing."

He laughed as he wrapped his bulky arms around her, holding her to his chest. "Silly Alice, men don't give birth. We do have mothers. What I mean to say is our women always give birth to males. It is genetically impossible for a woman to give birth to a girl child if she mates with one of our species. The baby will always be male."

Alice nodded, trying to ignore her beating heart. Everything he was telling her seemed to have come out of a creepy sci-fi movie. But strangely, she was interested in hearing more, especially if she ever wanted a chance to escape and return to Earth. "So, you only, uh, have sex with human females?"

"Yes, your genetics are the closest to ours, which makes impregnating your kind easy. We've tried with other species, but human females are the more docile creatures and perfect for childrearing, since we are often in the battlefield. Though they are rather delicate."

"Which means you can easily bully us into submission," she grumbled.

Kyvan, however, didn't look annoyed like the king had; he looked amused. "Our people have been doing this for centuries, picking up human females, which is why we have our other form as well." He transformed briefly into his alien form with its sharp teeth, gray skin, and red eyes. When he saw Alice tremble, he returned to his human form. "Half and half. Part of our mother and our father, it is quite interesting if you think about it."

"Best thing I've heard in my entire life," she quipped sarcastically. Her blue eyes widened. "Wait, does this mean aliens have been stealing women from Earth for centuries?"

He nodded. "In recent years, we have had to be more careful, with all the technology humans have created. Memory erasing is a hassle. King Korrev has made us study the females closely before we take them back home. To only choose those who have the disposition of being lonely, to not raise the alarm." Alice had to pretend his words didn't hurt. "Once, we took many women from a drinking establishment. We later found out they preferred female sex organs as well. They put up quite a fight, so we had to erase their memories and return them. The king was furious."

"You raided a lesbian bar?" she blurted out.

A twitch of a smile played on his lips. "Unintentionally. As you can see, we have learned from our mistakes. You, being the prime example."

"How flattering." Alice looked up at him. "What about you? Do you… did you have a mom?"

A sad look appeared briefly on his face before disappearing. "I did once. My father ended her life soon after my birth. She never coped with being taken and her sadness increased after the birth, to the point of neglecting me. My father thought he was doing her a kindness, as she wouldn't have survived our world if she continued like that and she was too far gone to be returned to Earth. He made it a quick and painless death, then he raised me by himself. The king and I grew up together, as playmates. He also grew up without a mother. My father is dead now. He died a warrior's dead in the time King Korrev's father was alive."

"He doesn't seem like a kind man."

"Warriors don't have the privilege of being kind, especially in the times we live in." Kyvan started stroking her dark hair. "These are times of peace compared to how things were, and I decided to focus my time on finding a mate who will give me children, which is where you come in, little Alice."

Alice gaped, her lower lip trembling. She had been expecting it based on where his storytelling was heading, but it was still a shock. Alice tried to stand up, but he was holding her firmly in his grasp.

"No, you c-can't," she stumbled over her words. "You said it yourself, we're delicate creatures. Besides, your kind live for a million years. Don't you want someone who lasts more than a second of your lifespan?"

He pressed a finger against her thigh. "The healer took care of that pesky business before I picked you up. We've found a chemical which will slow your aging tremendously. I'm only eight-nine now. Don't worry, little Alice. You and I will be together for decades to come. You're my mate. My partner. My life. I will make sure you and our offspring are safe. You only have to worry about getting round with my children." He smirked as he started nibbling her ear. His long tongue caressed the shell of her ear, which caused her to shiver deliciously. "Of which, there will be plenty. I would savor these few moments you are not with child if I were you, Alice."

The needle. She recalled the large needle which had caused a burning pain on her thigh. It had contained the cure to anti-aging all women strived for. Nice of them to let her know.

She swallowed. What if she never got out of here? She would be nothing more than a breeding machine he would constantly fill with his hot alien seed, No, it would never happen. Not on her watch. She might have a boring life on

Earth, but dammit, it was her life. No macho alien creature had the right to take it away from her.

"N-no."

He raised an eyebrow. "No?"

"No, I won't stay here to be your brood mare. I refuse to." Alice silently patted herself on the back for her bravery even though it was slowly diminishing, the more she looked at his green eyes.

"I'm afraid it's too late, Alice." He touched the blue bow against her neck which was starting to feel more like a hanging rope. "You will obey me, and that is final. You will not go back to Earth; there is nothing for you there. You will stay as my mate and the mother of my children. I swear to you, Alice, I will make you very happy."

Alice's first thought was to argue with him, but Kyvan didn't seem like the type to reason. He had kidnapped her, for God's sake! Perhaps it would be foolish to run, but she had to at least try. She would regret it forever if she took the coward's way out.

Her legs started moving before her brain had a chance to catch up. Her fingers had barely touched the door handle when she felt a strong but gentle grip around her neck, as if she were a disobedient kitten, before being pulled back.

A pained yelp escaped from her lips and his grip on her loosened. He flipped her around so she was facing him, her small breasts nearly being crushed against his hard chest. Alice could practically hear him breathing heavily, but she forced herself not to lower her trembling chin.

Kyvan's green eyes flashed with annoyance. "That was very naughty, Alice. Get this through your stubborn head. You cannot, and will never, escape me. I will fight to my last breath to prevent it from ever happening."

Alice spit on him while he still had the hard grip on the back of her neck. Kyvan didn't even blink, he looked more annoyed than anything. "You shouldn't have done that, my little troublemaker, now I have to punish you."

"I don't care," Alice spat. "You can beat me, starve me, hang me by my ankles, and I still won't—"

"I'm going to spank you," he said, interrupting her monologue and catching her completely by surprise.

Alice blinked her blue eyes. "Spank me? Like a child?"

Kyvan nodded gravely, like he had said nothing out of the ordinary. "Our species have been studying humans for a long time, especially females who are our breeding partners. A spanking is a perfect punishment for when you are disobedient. It helps you learn your lesson, and now you will learn your place. You will obey me, Alice Andrews, it's up to you how sore your bottom will be when you finally decide to do as you're told."

"N-no." Alice didn't know why, but she would rather take the beating or the starvation. A spanking was just too humiliating, too dehumanizing. She would never be able to hold her head up high if she were spanked like a naughty girl.

Kyvan looked unfazed as he quickly used the hold he had on the back of her neck to place her over his hard knee as if she weighed no more than a pillow. The jackass wasn't even sitting down to deliver her punishment; instead, he remained standing while she lay naked over his raised knee awaiting her punishment.

Alice squirmed as she felt her boobs bounce lewdly in the air while his other hand was placed on her lower back firmly, to keep her in place. She whimpered as she looked at him pleadingly with her big eyes. She was never one to play the part of a damsel in distress, but she quickly changed her tune when it was her own ass, literally, on the line.

However, her captor looked less than sympathetic, a whole different person from the college Kyvan, who had worshipped at her feet and followed her around like a lovesick puppy. Apparently, it had all been an act and he wasn't so easily fooled.

"Your actions caused this, troublemaker. You have no one to blame but yourself."

Before she could argue with him, his large, heavy palm landed on her upturned cheeks, causing Alice to cry out as she felt the immediate sting. His hand hurt! She was barely acknowledging the sting when it fell again. Kyvan's hand was large enough for it to land on both of her butt cheeks simultaneously.

She felt her cheeks bounce in the air as they slapped against each other with each movement of his heavy hand. Alice felt her bottom grow hotter and hotter, the more he peppered her cheeks, seemingly trying to get every inch of her pale bottom to turn a crimson red.

"Stop it!" she yelped when Kyvan landed a particularly hard slap against the back of her thighs, leaving behind a stinging sensation. "Stop it, right now."

He ignored her and, instead, continued to focus on turning her ass into a hot, red mess. Tears started forming in her eyes and despite the fact she wanted to prevent them from falling, she lost the battle, the longer the spanking continued.

Alice felt a burning sensation coming from her bottom, already dreading sitting and simply walking for the next couple of days. Or perhaps she would always find herself sleeping on her belly from now on, given his need to spank the disobedience out of her.

She didn't know how many times Kyvan landed his hand on her jiggling cheeks. But when the spanking became too much and she realized his hand continued to fall despite her protests, she finally submitted to him as she lay limply over his knees crying her eyes out.

Kyvan finished tanning her hide when he noticed Alice

had finally submitted to her punishment. The room was silent, the only sound coming from a mixture of her tears and the loud slaps which echoed from the small living quarters.

Despite his harsh punishment, Alice couldn't ignore the burning sensation she felt growing between her legs as Kyvan started rubbing her ass roughly, his fingers pressing against the welts he had caused as if studying them.

Alice pressed her thighs together once she felt his hand lowering to her pussy. Infuriatingly enough, she could feel her wetness coating her lower lips. Her dewy lips were stuck together with her juices as if humbly preparing itself for Kyvan's dick. What was wrong with her that her body was turned on despite being spanked to tears?

"Good girl," Kyvan murmured as he pinched a bit of a sore buttock between his fingers, causing her to moan. "Your punishment is over, little Alice."

Alice continued sobbing over his knee long after he stopped spanking her. She barely acknowledged him as he continued to rub the sting away from the beaten cheeks. Was this her life now, filled with punishment spankings and being bred?

Whimpers escaped her lips as he removed her from his knee, convinced he was going to fuck her next so they could start the baby making process he seemed so desperate for. But he didn't.

Instead, he wrapped an arm around her waist, pressing her against his body, as if he were carrying a sack of pota-toes, and headed to what she presumed was the living room. He then placed her on her knees, facing the wall, with the balls of her feet pressing against her sore little cheeks.

Alice looked at him, confused, not daring to move.

"Corner time," Kyvan announced gruffly, folding his arms over his bulky, smooth chest. "For fifteen minutes, so you can think about your actions which led you here and for you to make peace with your situation. Then I'm going to put you down for a nap. I think you're overstimulated and need some quiet time. This is your new life, Alice."

He kissed the back of her head, before he disappeared to make sure all the security protocols were heavily placed, leaving Alice behind to think about her situation and her well-spanked bottom.

Chapter 4

ALICE MUST HAVE BEEN MORE exhausted than she had realized, because as soon as Kyvan picked her up from corner time, he deposited her on her belly on his large bed with gentleness she was sure was fake because of how rough he had been earlier.

She hadn't planned to fall asleep, but as soon as he had put her to bed while landing a kiss on her forehead, Alice had gone to sleep very quickly. Maybe it was because of how much she had cried or because of how exhausted she had been between the kidnapping and learning her only job until she died was to produce heirs.

When she awoke, a quick peek out the window told her it was night outside. She tried pulling open the windows even though they were several floors up, but it seemed they had been glued shut.

Alice was still naked, the blue bow around her neck being the only accessory she had on her and she desperately wanted clothes. She felt extremely vulnerable and she did not like it.

Currently, she was inspecting her well-spanked bottom in

the mirror. Her ass was a deep, cranberry red which was still hot to the touch despite the fact it had been hours since she had been spanked. There was an array of welts from where Kyvan's punishing hand had landed the most, mainly in the center of her cheeks. The welts were mostly a dark pink, but one or two had a light violet shade which she knew would stick around for days.

Alice winced when she pressed a finger against the smallest welt she could find. Ow. Kyvan could definitely deliver a punishment. At this point, Alice would agree to anything if it meant he wouldn't spank her again. But then again, who was she kidding? Alice's mouth always seemed to get her in trouble, especially when she was annoyed.

The door opened, letting Kyvan in. He was holding a tray that carried some kind of orange soup and a glass of water. Alice immediately stopped inspecting her bottom to turn and face him with a scowl on her face.

Kyvan seemed ignorant of her annoyance. Instead, he placed the tray on the night table and pointed to the bed. "Come eat, Alice."

"I'm not hungry." Alice sulked.

Kyvan raised an eyebrow. "Must I punish you so soon after your spanking? You promised you would be a good girl from now on. You need to eat and drink some water. I've read it's important for humans to drink water, especially after crying sessions, or you risk dehydration."

"In all this reading you seem to do, wasn't there a chapter on how you don't spank adult women you kidnapped and forced as your mate?" Alice asked sarcastically.

Kyvan ignored her. He grabbed her by the wrist and pulled her towards him. When he sat down on the bed, Kyvan immediately wrapped an arm around her waist before he placed her firmly on his lap, her sore nates receiving an abrupt welcoming.

Alice squealed out in pain. "Kyvan! I'm still sore, I don't want to be sitting."

"Then you should have listened the first time." Kyvan and Alice were sitting so close together, the tips of her breasts were nearly rubbing against his naked chest. For an alien warrior, he smelled nice, like pine trees.

No, Alice, focus, she scolded herself, but her body seemed to have other plans as she felt a familiar throbbing sensation, followed by warm moisture slowly starting to drip. She bit back a groan. At this rate, by the time dinner was over, she would be coating his entire thigh with her juices.

Kyvan raised the glass of water to her lips, ordering firmly, "Drink."

Alice thought about throwing a tantrum, but where would it get her? She did not want another spanked bottom. Instead, she opened her mouth slowly, and once the first taste of water hit her dry tongue ,she started drinking it as if she were going to die of thirst.

"Easy." Kyvan smiled as he lowered the glass slightly so she wouldn't spill any on herself. "Good girl. Drink more, Alice."

Once Alice finished drinking her water, her muscles relaxed slightly as she practically curled her head against the crook of his neck. Kyvan placed down the empty glass of water and reached for the bowl of soup.

Alice wrinkled her nose like a picky child. "What is it? The color is weird."

He laughed. "It is a traditional dish, much better for you than your greasy human food. Just try it, sweetheart."

Alice hesitated, and the only reason she didn't push him away was because she was hungry. She opened her mouth slightly as he placed the spoon inside her mouth. "Very good, my little troublemaker."

A hint of color spread through her cheeks at his praise. It

shouldn't feel as good, given that he'd kidnapped her, but his voice was so annoyingly soothing, it was hard not to want to hear him sound happy with her, instead of exasperated.

She opened her mouth for another spoonful. He was right; it didn't taste bad. It reminded her of carrot soup, but much sweeter. She felt his hand underneath her breast to hold her steady.

His thumb rubbed softly against her erect nipple, causing the pink bud to harden against his finger while his remaining fingers caressed the soft flesh of her boob. Alice pressed her legs together, hardly paying attention to the dinner anymore, instead, only focusing on his wandering fingers. Kyvan was barely touching her, and here she was, ready to go down on all fours like a bitch in heat.

"Open your mouth, do not be distracted," Kyvan scolded slightly as he managed to slip her another spoonful while he squeezed her breast slightly.

Alice managed three more spoonsful before she addressed the elephant in the room. "Kyvan?"

"Yes, little Alice?"

"Please let me go."

Pause.

"I'm afraid it won't be possible. You are my mate. I chose you, you have my name imprinted on your bottom and my collar around your neck. You are my property. I cannot just let you go."

Alice's eyes watered, her lower lip trembling at the same time. "Please let me go, Kyvan. I never agreed to this. Let me return to Earth. There were dozens of girls in the room. Choose one of them to be your mate. I'm sure they would be dying to have someone like you."

So what if what she was saying was selfish? Survival of the fittest.

Kyvan stuffed the spoon in her mouth one final time. He

had a serious expression on his face, looking at her intensely. He didn't look angry, but it was clear he was not going to be swayed by her cries or begging. "I do not want anyone but you. Alice, make peace with the idea that you can never escape me." He gave her a wry smile. "Perhaps in death. Do you have what it takes to kill me, little Alice?"

Alice pursed her lips. "Don't count me out. I may surprise you yet."

Kyvan smiled at her as if she were a child threatening him. He kissed the tip of her nose. "Do you want more food or water?"

She shook her head as he started cleaning up. "Kyvan," Alice said again, "you cannot spank me when you think I've misbehaved. Punishing a grown woman like that is childish, no matter what you studied."

"But it works," Kyvan rebutted calmly as he stopped at the doorway. "Spanking has been used as a method of discipline for unruly females ever since we started bringing human females down to mate. It helps you learn your lesson, Alice. You are too headstrong and independent when you no longer have to be." She scowled, and he winked at her. "Besides, if you're good, you have nothing to worry about. I do not discipline on purpose. If you're good, you will be rewarded."

"Rewarded, how? With my freedom?"

"I'll think of something. Being rude, will get you nowhere, Alice. Just a thought."

He turned to head to the kitchen, and that's when Alice saw his back. While his front was full muscle, with a glistening six pack, his back was covered with old scars, some white with age, others fresh, with the dark red color barely settling in.

Once he came back, he raised an eyebrow when he saw her staring at him with wide eyes. "What?"

"Your back." She gulped. "It full of scars. Are you often hurt?"

He chuckled as he sat next to her on the large bed. He pressed a large hand against her scalp. It felt oddly comforting. "Do not worry about me, Alice. I am a warrior. I bear these scars proudly. It proves to me and everyone else I am not a coward. I will protect my planet and my woman with my life if necessary."

Alice didn't say anything. If Kyvan died, then what would happen to her? Would she be sent back, or would she simply be transferred to someone else?

Kyvan placed his hands on her hips, not giving her another chance to answer. He twisted her around so she was on all fours, doggy-style. Her chest was pushed against the mattress while her sore rump was in the air as if begging for another spanking.

"What are you doing?" she asked, feeling terribly exposed.

"Now, we mate." Kyvan's expression was calm, as if he were talking about another chore they had to do. He removed his underclothing, exposing his nudity. Alice felt her entire body grow hot. This was the first time she had seen a man naked—well, half-man—outside of porn. Kyvan's thighs were easily the size of half her body, while his cock, which was glistening with its precum, was nestled between them, growing larger, the more Alice stared at it. "It's the only way for us to mate."

"I know that!" she snarled. "Did you not hear our earlier conversation. I do not want to be your mate. I do not want a child, therefore, this whole mating process cannot occur."

She squeaked when she felt his large index finger part her love lips open, exposing her dewy center like a ripe, juicy peach. "Your body says otherwise, my little troublemaker," he murmured as he moved his finger up and down her slit, causing her legs to clench and her traitorous hips to move forward, as if begging for more. "Now be a good girl, Alice. The healer told me you are an untouched maiden. I promise I will be very gentle with you. Your body was made for this; look how it responds to my fingers."

"But I don't—" She couldn't even finish her sentence before a groan escaped through her lips as he started stroking her faster, making her wetter and wetter. Her legs were now spread fully apart, exposing every inch of her needy pussy.

Alice had masturbated before, but it had never felt like this. To be touched by someone else, even an asshole alien warrior, was positively wonderful.

"Don't lie," he scolded her as he landed a slap on her already sore ass. "Especially when you already squirted for me."

Horrified, she turned her head, expecting Kyvan to be lying, but he wasn't. His lower lip and chin were covered with her juices which must have escaped her lower body. Heat erupted throughout her whole body as she saw him lick the remnants of her juices with his long, pink tongue, like a venomous snake overlooking his prey.

She whimpered before she buried her face against the mattress. She wanted to tell him to stop, to leave her alone, but at the same time, her body was desperate for his touch. The throbbing sensation had grown rapidly ever since he'd started playing with her body.

Kyvan started kissing her lower back and then her seared cheeks, before he parted her ass open. Alice clutched the bed sheets desperately. He wasn't going to start there, was he? One of his fingers started pressing against her engorged clit and began rubbing it in rapid strokes, causing shocks of pleasure to bolt through her body almost immediately.

A thick finger was pressing against her pink rosebud. "One day, your little hole will be mine, but for now, we will start with your cunt." He cupped her heated pussy in his hand.

Alice didn't say anything; it was like the earth had stayed still. Kyvan gripped her hair with his hand as he plunged into her while he pushed her forward. Alice gasped when his cock pierced into her rapidly. She felt a sharp pain in her midsection as he tore through her virginity with his manhood.

Her eyes watered as he started playing with her breasts, alternating between squeezing them gently and rubbing her hardened pink nipples between his fingers. Kyvan kissed the back of her head. "There, troublemaker, the problem of your virginity has been taken care of." He showed her his dick covered with her virginal blood, which was now dripping down onto the sheets.

She glared at him angrily as she stared at his bloodied cock. Kyvan's hand was still stroking her breasts. The anger left her eyes when he leaned forward and dug his sharp teeth against one of her breasts. The pain was sharp, but at the same time, it felt good.

Alice groaned, her anger temporarily forgotten as she focused on the way he was torturing and teasing her breasts as he bit at the sensitive nips, only to caress them with his tongue a few seconds later.

Once he saw she was relaxed once again, he gripped her hips and plunged into her again. This time, Alice did not complain as he buried his cock inside her, spreading her walls as he filled her.

Alice's breasts bounced in the air as he fucked her, his fingers refusing to leave her clit which was growing more overstimulated by the second. Moans filled the room—he felt good. Alice didn't want it to feel good. He had kidnapped her, for God's sake!

But it didn't just feel good, it felt extraordinary. Skin met skin as one of his hands dug against her hips. Their hips bounced against each other while he thrust into her and Alice shamelessly rubbed her sore ass against his thighs.

She felt her orgasm hit her vividly as her body temperature rose, causing goosebumps to cover her arms when Kyvan came inside her. His hot seed slipped out of her body and onto the back of her thighs and sheets while her shoulders relaxed.

Kyvan landed a slap against her ass as Alice lay limply, face down on the bed, her heart nearly bursting inside her chest. Kyvan faced her as he pushed a long, dark strand away from her face. He kissed the tip of her nose. "That wasn't so terrible, was it, little Alice?"

Alice didn't answer. If she admitted it wasn't bad, then it would just serve as a green light for him to do whatever he wanted. Not that he had to ask for permission, given that, apparently, she was his mate.

Kyvan and Alice remained lying down quietly for a few minutes, to the point she was starting to fall asleep. Then, suddenly, he sat up. "That's enough resting."

Before Alice could ask him what he meant, Kyvan had once again grabbed her by her hips easily, lifted her, and sat her down on the mushroom head of his cock which was still covered in a mixture of his cum and her blood.

Alice yelped as she straddled him, her sore buttocks hitting his hard thighs every time he thrust into her. She placed her hands on top of his shoulder blades to steady herself. He bit her earlobe gently. "Do not worry, Alice, I will never let you fall."

"Because you want to do the pushing?" she managed to ask as her boobs bounced with the rhythm of his strokes, nearly hitting him against the face, which would no doubt please the asshole.

Kyvan pressed both of his hands against her spanked

cheeks, his fingers gripping the punished flesh as he rubbed them against the welts he had placed there. Alice whimpered as he landed a kiss on her lips. "Because you're my most precious thing. You're my mate, and I will guard you with my life, my little troublemaker."

Alice forgot how many times he fucked her that night. All she knew, was that she went to bed feeling positively exhausted.

Chapter 5

ALICE REMAINED in Kyvan's quarters for two more days before he told her they were going out.

Alice's first thought was to continue giving him the cold shoulder, still furious he had dragged her away from her home without her consent. The only time it seemed she made any noise was when he was buried between her legs, with his large cock stretching her fully while his long, thin tongue licked away her tears when the sensations became too much from the constant array of orgasms he was giving her non-stop.

The young woman didn't even have a chance to feel sore, because she was barely getting used to the empty feeling before he was spreading her legs open, burying her face in the pillow while he entered her from behind.

It made Alice wonder how she had made it to twenty-two without ever having sex. If she knew it would feel this good, she would have lost her virginity a long time ago. Though she doubted human sex was as pleasurable as alien sex, given the complaints she had heard throughout the years about women not being able to achieve orgasm.

Alice never had a problem with Kyvan in that department. Sometimes she even had to beg him to let her get some rest, a fact which had confused him more than once when he seemed to forget she didn't have his crazy alien stamina. Every other complaint she had fell on deaf ears. When she was acting particularly bratty, Kyvan would just send her to the corner until she composed herself, or if it was bedtime, he would forcibly wrap his strong arms around her and place her against his chest while she cried tears of frustration until she fell asleep.

So far, she had managed to avoid another spanking. While she still groaned when she sat down, her bottom had returned to a baby pink color and was no longer crimson red. However, she knew as the days went by, there was a good chance Kyvan would no longer feel so generous.

But Alice couldn't just let it go. He had kidnapped her and taken her away from Earth forever. Was she supposed to just let it go?

"Where are we going?" she grumbled. "Back to Earth hopefully?"

Kyvan ignored her second statement. He was still shirtless but was wearing a pair of black shorts. Were all the aliens on this planet allergic to clothes, or what?

"You've been cooped up here for too long, it's making you unbearable. A little walk will do you good. Besides, you are due for a checkup with Azis."

"Azis?"

"The healer." He raised an eyebrow. "Unless you want to continue making a fuss. I could bring him here if that's the case."

"No," she blurted out. "I'll be good."

"Excellent. Let's go."

"Wait! I can't go out like this." She looked at her nude body, her ass still pink, hickies covering her neck and breasts, and traces of his fingertips decorating her skin. "I'm naked. I need clothes."

"You don't."

"What if I get cold?"

"It's not cold out."

"Do you want other men to see me naked? Do you plan to share me with your weird alien friends?"

Kyvan's face darkened at her taunt as he gripped her wrist, turning her around to point to her backside where his name was branded on her ass. "See this? The minute someone sees this, they know you're mine. They wouldn't dare go after my woman. If there is something men in this planet have, it is loyalty. Don't provoke me or them, Alice. I will gladly beat them to a bloody pulp if anyone dares touch you, and I'll make you watch. Now, let's go."

Alice crossed her arms stubbornly over her chest. "I'm not going without clothes."

He sighed. "I don't have any clothes for you, little one. The clothes I have are too big for you and the other is my suit of armor, which will bury you. If the idea of going out nude displeases you so much, I will just call the healer and—"

"No!" she blurted out. She couldn't lose the opportunity to get out of this hell hole. She was suffocating in here. Her eyes caught the long white sheet from the bed and she started pulling on it. "I'll just use this." She wrapped the sheet around her body like a long dress. It would be a pain to drag it, but it was better than being naked.

Kyvan shook his head as if he were dealing with a stubborn toddler. "Suit yourself. Let's go."

It turned out, as one of the king's most loyal warriors, Kyvan's quarters were located inside King Korrev's large palace. The palace was decorated in shades of gray and white, with lush pink and green gardens, endless doors, and statues depicting the king's late father, most of the time murdering an enemy.

Tiny blue creatures the size of raccoons, with bushy tails and large eyes, were scurrying across the palace. Kyvan called them timkes and said they were the palace workers, who kept the place clean and ran errands for the king or his warriors.

"Do they understand you?" Alice asked when she overhead a pair of them speaking in an odd language that not even her translator could depict. "Can you understand them?"

"Yes." Kyvan smiled as he pressed a hand on the small of her back protectively before pressing her against his side. "They're not really talkers, which makes them great servants. Korrev makes sure they are paid handsomely so they remain loyal."

Alice looked at the blue creatures again. They were kind of cute. Maybe Kyvan would let her keep one as a pet. She shook her head. What was she thinking? The plan was to get out of here, not settle into domestic life.

"I thought you were going to show me around Krotev?" she asked casually. "Not just around the palace."

Kyvan rubbed her shoulders. "Another time, little Alice."

Alice pouted. "You don't trust me, do you?"

"I think you need to know the palace first, and be comfortable with your situation, before you decide to venture outside of the palace walls."

"That's a fancy way of saying you don't trust me," Alice responded flatly.

Kyvan only answered by kissing the top of her head. Alice soon got distracted again when she saw the view a few feet away from her. Apparently, Kyvan had not been lying to her. In the distance, she saw three alien men with their mates. Alice could tell they were warriors like him because of their strong builds and former war wounds decorating their skin.

They were each with their mates who, unlike Alice, who was trying to cover her body with the sheet, were naked. One of them was a pretty woman around her age, with her hair in a long ponytail and glowing copper skin, who was being heavily petted as she and her mate sat on a bench giggling together like a couple of high-schoolers.

A heavier alien, with brown hair in a ponytail, was chasing a small Asian woman playfully in his alien form, in a cat and mouse game. Near the fountain, another woman, this one in her mid-twenties, with short brown hair, was getting spanked ruthlessly by her mate, whose name was also branded on one of her buttocks.

"They're naked," Alice made the comment before she turned around, trying to give the women some privacy even though it was obvious they didn't care who saw them nude.

"Women rarely wear clothes. A true warrior would never dream of touching another's mate. The offense is punishable by death after all." He kissed her cheek. "However, if you truly want clothes, I will get you a dress next time I'm at the market."

"Why a dress?" she mumbled as she turned her head once again to the couples. They were as gentle with them as Kyvan was with her, even if one was getting spanked like she had on her first day. "Why not a pair of jeans?

"A dress gives me easier access to you." He pulled her close teasingly. "And I love every part of you, Alice."

Alice blushed as she buried her face against the sheet. She wasn't used to being fawned over, then again, Kyvan had fawned over her since they first met. He led her away from the couples which she was grateful for, since she was starting to get secondhand embarrassment.

Her next destination turned out to be a place which

looked like a cave. It was very cold and made out of a brown, thick material with several beds. She shivered under her sheet as Kyvan explained the room was built this way to promote a faster route to health, as their species weakened somewhat in the heat. The cold helped their wounds heal quickly whenever they were stuck here after being injured in a fight.

This didn't make much sense to Alice, then again, very few things in this world did. An elderly alien who was only a few inches taller than she was, with a white goatee, was mumbling under his breath as he hunched over a beaker which held some sort of green liquid that Alice hoped she didn't have to swallow.

Unlike Kyvan and the rest of his alien friends, he was thankfully dressed from head to toe. He didn't look at all intimidating, like her mate or the king, which helped some-what. A timke was holding its chubby arms, which held several different-colored beakers, in the air.

"Azis." Kyvan cleared his throat as he pushed her slightly forward. "I have brought my mate for her checkup."

Azis gave both of them an annoyed look. Obviously, he didn't like being interrupted. "You're the sixth warrior who has brought me their mate today. I do have other things to do." He shook his head. "I don't often see you in your human form."

"She's been fussy, which is why we didn't come earlier." He shrugged as Alice scowled at him. "She is still fearful of my true form, which is why I remain like this."

You would be fearful, too, if I looked like a demon, Alice grumbled in her head as she forced a smile. She wouldn't be able to find a way back home if she made enemies everywhere. "Hi, pleased to meet you. I'm Alice Andrews."

"I know who you are." Azis pointed impatiently to the bed. "Strip and lie on the table, on all fours." He put on a pair of gloves and then rubbed some sort of clear liquid on them.

Alice hesitated as she clutched the sheet around her body. How many more people were going to see her nude today?

Azis gave her mate an irritated look. Kyvan threw her a warning look. "Alice, please do as Azis ordered, or you will be tied with your leash." Before they had left, Alice had seen him discreetly hide a pale blue leash in his bag which matched the bow around her neck. Apparently, being treated like a dog here was second nature to them.

She hesitated; she didn't want to be examined by Azis, but she also didn't want to be tied, or worse, spanked in front of this man. Alice let the sheet fall to the floor, exposing her nakedness as she made her way to the bed.

She placed herself on all fours like Azis had motioned, feeling like a prized calf. It reminded her of the position Kyvan had placed her in to rob her of her virginity a few days prior, except this position felt far less pleasant because she knew she was going to get prodded.

Even though her thighs were pressed tightly together, given her position, she was giving the healer a glimpse of all her female charms. Despite the shame she was feeling, she wasn't oblivious to the fact her nipples hardened with each of the alien's movements.

It was as if her body was wondering with anxious antici-pation what would happen next. Her breasts swung gently against each other as she heard the sharp sounds of blue leather gloves. Alice squealed when she felt Azis' large, meaty fingers parting her dewy lips open before he started to roughly fuck her with one finger before he added a second. He alternated between spreading her open as wide as he could and burying his fingers as deep as he could, causing a pained whimper to escape.

Alice tried to move away from him, but it seemed Azis

followed her as he gripped one plump butt cheek to keep her from moving. Kyvan placed one hand on top of her head and kissed her forehead gently. "You're doing fine, little Alice. Stay still now."

She pouted as Azis dug a third finger inside her, going as deep as he could. He then slowly pressed all three fingers inside her wet core. Alice tried to ignore her trembling thighs; if he continued acting the way he was, she was going to come all over his fingers.

"You broke her hymen." Azis sounded proud as he removed his hand. "She's tight, but she is inexperienced and unused. If anyone can break her in, it would be you, Kyvan." Kyvan patted Alice's cheek as she scowled.

Her scowl was soon removed from her face when her folds were parted again, and this time Azis' finger found her needy clit. He rubbed the little nub between his gloved fingers and started rubbing the sensitive bundle of nerves, making sure he touched every part of it.

Azis chuckled when her hips started bucking, nearly pressing her ass against his face as his fingers kept rubbing her weepy clit, her wetness leaking from her, going down her round thighs.

Alice's fingers clutched against her thighs, wishing she could rub her clit until she came, but she didn't know if it would upset her captors. At this point, she was so horny, she didn't care what either of them thought.

When she was close to the edge, Azis removed his hands from her clit before delivering a hard slap against her sore ass cheeks, causing it to bounce and a red handprint to appear on her ass. Alice moaned in both pain and despair. What was it with these masochist aliens who couldn't leave her ass alone?

"Your mate is very responsive, Kyvan. She is quite a lucky girl. There are some girls we need to give enhancement to, to make them feel something, but not her. A mere touch on her clit and her little cunny is practically weeping."

Alice felt like weeping right now. She didn't know how much of this humiliation she could take, especially when she was feeling so horny.

"She's a good girl," Kyvan praised as he ran a finger against his name engraved on her ass. "Most of the time, anyway. I'm planning on putting a lot of babies in her."

Alice blushed.

Azis nodded approvingly as he placed a hand on her lower back, forcing Alice to place her breasts against the bed while her red ass was raised, as if begging for another spanking.

"Spread her cheeks," he ordered to Kyvan as the alien warrior grabbed one meaty cheek in each hand, exposing her wide open. Her pink bottom hole twitched in the cool air at the sudden exposure.

"What are you doing?" Alice demanded nervously as she started wiggling around. "Stop it, right now! I never—"

Alice stopped when she felt something cool against her exposed anus before it was assaulted with Azis' large finger. Tears stung her eyes when she felt her butthole being violated for the first time. Even she didn't touch herself there, with the exception of when she was showering.

Azis started thrusting his finger in and out of her. She would barely sigh with relief when it was out before he was buried knuckles deep inside her ass. Unlike his previous ministration, this one didn't feel as enjoyable.

Kyvan tried to calm her by petting her gently, but it wasn't helping much. "She's very tight." Azis sounded disapproving as he finally removed his finger with a pop before he landed another slap against the opposing cheek so his two palm prints decorated her rear end. "You're going to have to loosen her up before you place your entire cock up her ass without breaking her. Thankfully, humans were clever enough to invent such devices."

Azis handed Kyvan a small box with an American brand Alice recognized. Apparently, even alien warriors weren't above shopping sprees. The box contained four different-sized butt plugs and a small bottle of lube. "This is a starter kit. Use some of these inside her before you fuck her from behind, though you'll never get a baby out of her that way, no matter how enjoyable it is."

Azis' hands then went towards her pale breasts as his fingers dug into the soft skin before he started twisting the pink nipples in his hands. "Breasts look nice and healthy. Has she gotten all of her shots?"

"Yes."

"Eating good?"

"Yes, she has quite an appetite. Though she was a bit picky about her food, I managed to convert her. Didn't I, Alice?"

"Sleeping at night?"

"Yes, I usually mate with her, which seems to tire her out. Human females don't have much energy."

"After five rounds of increased fucking, I would have to be a mutant not to feel tired." Alice narrowed her eyes crabbily. She was tired of playing show pony, especially since the two men were speaking about her as if she wasn't there.

The healer turned to her as if she were an inconvenience. "We're done here." He then turned back to Kyvan as both of them started guessing about how long it would take until her belly was swollen with child.

Alice's hands went towards her flat stomach, perspiration clinging to her skin no matter how cold the room was. No, this was not going to be her fate. She had a bright future ahead of her which did not include making babies non-stop.

The sheet was wrapped tightly around her as Azis led

Kyvan to a smaller room, no doubt to show him new torture devices to use in several parts of her body. This was her chance to run, the words were practically ringing in her ear. Kyvan hardly left her alone.

This might be her only chance before she was once again locked up in her glass cage. Her fingers touched the blue bow around her neck. It still had the tracker inside. Despite countless attempts, she still hadn't found a way to remove it from her neck.

She had a choice to make; she could either stay with Kyvan and figure out how to remove the bow first, or she could run and take her chances while figuring out how to remove the tracker along the way.

Perhaps it was desperation or sheer stupidity, but Alice choose the second option.

Run.

Chapter 6

WHERE AM I?

Damn, everything in this godforsaken planet looked exactly the same. It was as if she were trapped in a maze. She knew she was still in some part of the palace, as Kyvan had mentioned it was where their quarters were, along with the healer's room and the freak dungeon she had woken up in.

But where was the exit?

Alice had no idea what she was going to do once she discovered the exit. All she knew was if she took the first step, she was golden and everything else shouldn't be too hard, right?

She would manage what to do later, once she managed to exit the palace, which was free of guards and, best of all, Kyvan. She tried to ignore the guilt which was settling in her chest when she remembered how patient her new "mate" had been with her during the past few days, but then she remembered she should be in a college lecture hall, instead of running through some fancy hallways naked.

Alice regretted getting rid of the sheet earlier at the healer's, especially since she was already vulnerable, but the sheet would give her away more easily. She was so nervous, she could easily trip on her own two feet.

The more time that passed, the more nervous Alice felt. She opened door after door but found nothing but fancy rooms or rooms used for training, given all the odd weapons she found. It almost felt like the palace was empty, or at least this floor was.

Kyvan had mentioned the floor where they lived was known as the communal floor, which they shared with the king's other faithful warriors, but there were other private parts of the palace that were used solely by the king and could only be approached with an invitation.

Alice found it odd that such a powerful king would have such lax security, but based on their brief encounter, King Korrev was oafish and cruel. He would probably welcome any attempt of an assassination, only to have the opportunity to deal with them himself.

One more door, she told herself as she turned the knob. If there was no clear exit here, then she would have no choice but to start climbing through windows. Alice had expected the room to be empty, like all the other rooms had been. But it wasn't.

Alice was too shocked about what she was seeing, she didn't bother not making a sound. Instead, she allowed the loud gasp to escape her lips. The proper thing would be to look away from this particular scene, but her blue eyes just seemed to widen in disbelief.

The king sat on his silver throne which was decorated with bright jewels. He had a bored expression on his face as if he were listening to a terrible conversation. King Korrev was completely naked and he didn't seem at all embarrassed as his clothes lay messily against the arm of his throne.

The image alone would have been odd enough had the

king been alone, but he wasn't. A woman in her early thirties was between his legs. The woman had long blonde hair which reached the middle of her back, golden locks which reminded Alice of Goldilocks or Rapunzel.

Her body was just as nude as the king's, with the exception of the pale moons of her rear end which had been colored such a dark red color, Alice would be surprised if she could sit down without bursting into tears. The blonde's bottom appeared freshly spanked; it was a beet red color, with sharp switch marks overlapping each other.

Even though her back was turned, Alice could see her breasts, which were round and full like a pair of ripe melons. Her breasts were also marked with switch marks, but they were faded as if it had been a few days since her chest had been punished. Nipples the color of strawberries stood out against the pale skin.

She wore a bow around her neck similar to Alice's, but hers was bright pink, which oddly matched the color of her hardened nipples.

The woman was sucking on the king's cock eagerly, her cheeks becoming hollow, the faster she sucked as she moved her head up and down. King Korrev pushed into her mouth lazily, forcing her small mouth to accept the last remaining inches.

The busty beauty's eyes watered at the sudden invasion as a choking sound escaped her mouth. She glared angrily at the king, something she doubted even the king's own warriors would do.

King Korrev simply raised an eyebrow, warning her. "Suck. Unless you want me to use your other entrance with only your spit as lubricant."

Her shoulders slumped as she continued sucking, her breasts heaving up and down as she got comfortable with his erect member in her mouth. In a rare moment of affection, King Korrev stroked her blonde hair. "Good choice, Karin."

Alice started to slowly move back to the door. The king seemed to be busy with his own mate; maybe she could go back without being noticed.

"Stop." King Korrev's voice rang out harshly, harsher than Kyvan's had ever been. "Stop walking and come forward."

Alice hesitated.

A cruel smirk appeared on the king's face. "Unless you want to be in the same place my Karin is right now." The blonde woman, apparently Karin, threw the king a hurtful expression which he promptly ignored.

Alice shook her head and quickly did as she was told. Once she was facing him, he instructed her in a bored voice, "Bend over."

The brunette quickly did as she was told, not wanting to find herself in Karin's predicament. Her cheeks turned red as she exposed her pink buttocks and hairless quim to yet another stranger.

King Korrev looked at her butt for what seemed like hours before he clicked his tongue. "Stand up. You're Kyvan's brat. I figured. I would have thought he would have a tighter hold on you."

"I didn't expect her to be so mischievous."

Alice blinked as she turned around. Kyvan was glaring at her angrily. He was in his true form, complete with the gray body and sharp teeth, which made him look like a demon. Alice stood frozen in place, unable to move, but despite her fear, her desire was seeping down her legs. There was just something about his molten stare which caused her womanhood to clench with need, as if her body was crying for him.

Kyvan reached her in four easy steps and quickly attached a leash on her before she could utter a single protest. She turned back to King Korrev and Karin, silently asking for help, but she received none.

Karin now laid her head on King Korrev's thigh sleepily while the king ran a hand through her luscious blonde locks in an almost affectionate way, despite how he was treating her earlier.

"Keep her on a tighter leash, Kyvan. I don't like being interrupted."

Kyvan nodded as he bowed to the king with his hand still around the nape of her neck, stirring her in the opposite direction.

Alice look back at Karin as if silently asking for help, but the blonde was already half asleep. "Kyvan."

"Stop talking," he hissed at her as he led her away, back to their home. He didn't speak the entire walk. Alice even forgot about her nudeness, because all she could think about was how sore her ass was going to be once he got her home.

Alice flinched when the door of his quarters locked behind her and he put in the code to make sure there wasn't a chance she would run away again. Her bottom lip trembled when he turned to face her angrily. He looked much more terrifying in his true form.

Alice hadn't really been terrified until this moment, as he had been gentle with her in his own weird way despite the spanks he gave her. He was still holding tightly to her leash as if secretly warning her that running away was pointless.

He finally removed the leash, which helped Alice relax somewhat. Her fingers touched the bow on her neck, hoping it could be removed as well. When she looked back up, she realized Kyvan was just inches away from her.

The alien held the back of her nape tightly, forcing her to look at him, but also silently reinforcing he was the one in charge. "Was I not clear before, little Alice?" he demanded as his fingers traced her nipples softly.

The pink traitors immediately tightened into tight little buds as a shiver ran down her spine. He squeezed one of her breasts and despite her better judgment, she rubbed her thighs together.

"Did you really think you could outrun me?" He squeezed her nape harder.

It took every ounce of Alice's self-restraint not to spit on him, trying to save her butt from a worse fate.

"N-no."

His hold relaxed somewhat. "Then, why did you run?"

"I had to try."

Kyvan chuckled at her honesty, but he didn't look the least bit amused. "Well, no creature is truly tamed, especially at the beginning." The next few words made Alice's body run cold. "I'm going to have so much fun breaking you, Alice. When I'm through with you, escaping from me will be the last thing on your mind."

He twisted one nipple harshly between his large thumb and finger and she let out a cry. "I thought you were nice!"

"I wanted to do things the nice way, but it seems, my Alice, you don't respond to niceness." His long, pink, snake-like tongue curled around her ear. "That's all right; if you respond better to a stronger hand, I am more than happy to oblige."

Kyvan removed his tongue from the shell of her ear and Alice looked at it with longing. He then gripped her wrist and pulled her towards his bedroom. While he used one hand to hold her upper arm, he used the other to pull forward a long, thin, pillowy bench that reminded her of the balance beam gymnasts used.

With one quick pull of her wrist, he draped her over the beam, buck naked, her breasts being crushed against the pillowy center. Alice barely captured what was going on when she found her arms and legs being tied to small hooks at the bottom of this newfound torture device.

"I don't want another spanking," she hissed at him as she tried to pull away, even though she knew it was useless.

"Then you shouldn't have run away." Kyvan did not seem concerned at all about her tantrum as he opened a drawer and pulled out a short, thin crop, like the kind used on horses. When Alice saw it, she started moving faster, like a fish out of water. The crop landed harshly on the center of her ass, which caused her moves to stop and a groan to escape. "Stop moving, unless you want my crop to land somewhere else." He devilishly pressed the edge of the crop against her wet pussy lips which seemed to be crying for him by the way they wept moisture every time he came near her.

Perhaps these alien freaks had injected her with something which made the body instantly horny every time he got closer to her.

"You're a psycho," Alice snarled at him, not caring if he punished her more severely, her butt already burning. "Are you going to spank me for every little thing? Aren't I supposed to be your mate?"

"As my mate, it is expected you remain obedient to me. So far, Alice, you have been acting like an incredibly naughty girl."

"Gee, I wonder why? Perhaps it's because you kidnapped me!"

"As for the spanking, you can expect an implement on your ass every time you disobey me." He smirked when he entered one finger inside her dewy core. A moan escaped her lips when he pushed it in deeper. "Though your body seems to like it even through your protests."

Her face heated. "I do not."

"We can discuss it later." Kyvan pulled out of her, leaving behind an empty feeling. "Now, it's time for your punishment, Alice. I hope you remember how your ass feels next time you think about disobeying me."

Before she could utter another protest, the implement fell rapidly on her soft skin. The riding crop dug harshly against the plump flesh, leaving behind a horrible, stinging feeling. Alice yelped as she tried to pull away, which proved fruitless, given that she was tied.

Instead, her butt was presented in such a way, it was like she was begging for punishment. The crop fell again, this time a little lower from where he had delivered the first stroke. Alice felt the puffy, pink line develop, the second Kyvan pulled the crop away.

She chewed on her bottom lip. Great, not only would she be sore for days, but the riding crop would leave faint lines and welts which would adorn her bottom for days and would eventually grow itchy.

For the next few minutes, she could only hear the sound of the riding crop slashing in the wind before it met tender skin, followed by her occasional moans. Alice tried her best not to cry, but it was nearly impossible with the way Kyvan was whipping her with firmness, making sure no part of her skin was left untouched.

The crop landed on every inch of her bottom, decorating the sensitive skin with long, pink, white, and red strokes against bouncing cheeks. Once or twice, Kyvan landed the stinging riding crop against her pussy lips, which were spread open because of the way she lamely tried to get away from him.

The pout of her sex swelled when it met the devilish crop and Alice wanted nothing more than to rub the sting away. Her ass was an angry red mess, and the more she moved her legs, the more the sore skin stretched, which only made her cry harder.

Her tears didn't seem to do much to her mate despite

how much he claimed to cherish her, as his lashes never lessened, even when she begged him to stop. He never made her bleed or bruised her porcelain skin, but he made sure she was a very sore little girl who wouldn't be able to sit down without wincing.

Alice was so busy crying, she hardly noticed when Kyvan pulled back the hair stuck to her sweaty forehead. He kissed her forehead, even though she was out of breath, before he ruffled her dark locks.

"Good girl, Alice. You took your punishment well. Now, just one more piece of your punishment, then we'll be done."

"Fuck you! You're not getting anywhere near my ass ever again."

Kyvan ignored her statement, obviously not caring about her protest. He opened the butt plug case the healer had given him earlier, picking the smaller one. Alice felt her sore cheeks being pulled open.

Her tight pink rosebud winked at him under the observation of his sharp eyes before he covered her bottom hole generously with lubricant. Alice wailed as he inserted the matching blue butt plug inside her hole little by little, until it was fully trapped inside. It didn't hurt, as he was being incredibly gentle, but she cried because it was so embarrassing.

Just a few days ago, she had been a witty, independent young college student, and now, she had been reduced to being someone's mate who was expected to be obedient, otherwise, she would sprout a bright red ass.

Alice had never felt so low.

There wasn't even a point in fighting him because he was stronger and would win every time. The plug felt funny in her rear end; it didn't hurt exactly, but she felt uncomfortably full and she grew unsuccessful in trying to push it out.

Kyvan untied her, then wrapped an arm around her

waist, pulling her up as if she were nothing more than a sack of potatoes. He tossed her gently on the bed. "Sleep. You're tired out. Maybe it will help your foul mood."

"Take it out," she cried out, her hand reaching for the plug, in spite of the fact that every move she made seemed to make it sink even deeper.

Kyvan slapped her hand away gently as he used his thumb to push the plug in even deeper, to make it less easy for her to remove it. "No, my little troublemaker. You'll sleep with it, to pay for your disobedience and to stretch you out." He raised an eyebrow. "Unless you want me to fill your hole with my cock right now. It is the only way I will remove it tonight, Alice. Do you want that?"

Alice shook her head, the tears streaming down her face as she cradled her poor, aching cheeks. She rested on her belly, not caring he had full view of her ass and how it was stretched out by the plug.

"I hate you! I despise you! I will get out of this hell hole, Kyvan! Mark my words." She didn't care if her comments earned her another spanking.

If Kyvan seemed upset by her words, he didn't show it. Instead, he lay down next to her, stroking her dark hair until she eventually fell into a deep slumber.

Chapter 7

ALICE WAS BORED.

When she wasn't pouting like a brat or giving Kyvan evil glares that promised mass destruction, which he thought was beyond adorable, she had no trouble telling him how she was feeling—bored out of her mind.

When one acquired a mate, King Korrev was unusually generous and gave each of his warriors three months of free time so they could train and bond with their mates, before he required them to rejoin his services and sent them into battle.

It had been three weeks since Kyvan had dragged Alice to his home planet after she showed him she had no desire to remain exclusive to him on Earth. It might as well have been only a day for the little progress they had made.

Alice was just as stubborn, harsh, and surly as when he had chosen her for his mate as a present from the king for a job well done. The tiny brunette hardly seemed to stand him even though he often made her cry out in pleasure while her entire body shook uncontrollably every time he mated with her.

It was clear her body liked what he did to her, but Alice

was another story. While she would cling to him and moan his name when he was on top of her or fucking her against the walls or decorating her hips with his finger marks as he entered her on all fours, as soon as the orgasm left her body, she would return to her cold treatment.

Kyvan wasn't sure why she was sad, exactly. While Earth was pleasant, it was no better than his home planet, and as far as he knew, Alice had no family and very few friends, which made it impossible for him to guess what she was missing.

Still, he was worried about her, especially when she would just curl on the bed, not moving and with tears in her eyes. It reminded him too much of his own mother, whom his father had to put to sleep because she had suffered from a crippling depression. He didn't want that to happen to Alice, but he didn't want to let her go, either, as selfish as it sounded.

Alice was his mate. He cared for her and he was sure he could convince her to care for him as well if she would just give him a chance. They couldn't remain the rest of their lives in complete silence.

"What?" Alice demanded as she looked up from the pillow which she was currently hugging against her chest after breakfast. The couch was large, to fit his larger frame, and she looked positively tiny on it. "Are you going to fuck me again?"

Alice didn't bother wearing his clothes anymore when it was clear Kyvan spent more time mounting her than it took her to get dressed. She had gotten used to walking around naked and no longer hid or covered herself with her hands.

It still remained a mystery to Kyvan why human females covered their bodies when they were so beautiful. Though Alice had mentioned human males were far less respectful when it came to other's "mates" than aliens.

"You're crabby." Kyvan didn't bother answering her question as he removed the pillow she was clutching to expose her bare breasts. Her nipples were pink and hard like they always were when she was around Kyvan, which always left her feeling terribly achy and sore. "I have a way to remedy that."

Alice threw him a dark look. "It had better not be a spanking or you filing me with your thing." She pointed to his erection which was growing bigger, the longer he stared at her breasts. His body was addicted to her, and if she wasn't a human who needed constant rest, he doubted he would ever leave her body. "I'm sore. You were on me for hours yesterday."

He gave a little shrug as he grabbed her by both of her ankles and pulled her to the edge of the bed until her legs were dangling. Kyvan spread her legs open, exposing her small pink quim which was sore from the constant stimulation. Her mate didn't even bother wearing clothes in their living quarters anymore because he was always on her in one way or another, trying to breed her.

Kyvan often tired her out, until Alice's only thoughts were devoted to sleep, which she was starting to believe was the plan all along. He might have fooled her with the puppy dog persona in the past, but he was smart, much smarter than he let on. He didn't become the king's right-hand man by being an airhead.

"You seem to enjoy it. You were hoarse by the end of the night." He grinned at her as he pointed to the faint fingernail marks she had left behind when he brought her to her orgasm for the fifth time in a row. Alice's legs had been draped around his waist as he fucked her with his cock, which made his shoulder blades her primary target.

After he made her come, he had tucked her in and kissed her forehead. Alice wondered how he could be so gentle with her and so strict when he was paddling her rump as he was delivering punishment.

Alice felt her cheeks grow red as she tried to say in a haughty tone, "I was going to scratch your eyeballs out, but I didn't want to die in your apartment without knowing the code to get out."

"You can scratch me as much as you want. Your little human nails are no match for my skin, it's much thicker than yours, to protect against injuries. It's the same reason why I don't get as cold as often as you do."

"Did you ever think about mating with other aliens instead of us, since we're so weak and frail compared to you?" Alice raised an eyebrow. "Or are you like a wolf chasing down a rabbit? Easily entertained."

"I am not sure what a wolf or a rabbit is, Alice. All I know is I find human females beautiful. Members of our planet have for as long as I can remember. Once we started mating with humans, we never stopped. My parents' own mating was a tragic story, but our bonds between humans have worked well in our favor, even if females have been a bit resilient at first." Kyvan reached a large hand to stroke her face. Alice found herself sinking her cheek against his calloused hand. "Since the moment I saw you, I knew I had to have you for myself. So, hate me all you want, yell at me, punish me, but it will not stop the attraction I have for you. You're mine, Alice, until the end of time, or until I die protecting you with an honorable warrior's death."

Kyvan was one of the king's warriors, and if history, combined with romance books, had taught her anything, it was that he was required to give up his life for the king if the situation required it.

That scenario should have made her feel glad. It would be a big "fuck you" to the man who had basically kidnapped her from her home. But it strangely made her feel sad. Yes, she wasn't Kyvan's biggest fan, but it didn't mean she wanted him dead, either. The thought of him dying in battle made her squeamish.

After the three months of her "taming" period were over, he was expected to return to King Korrev's side. She bit her lower lip. "What if you die? What happens to me?"

Kyvan smirked at her, tilting his head as if the pair were at a coffee shop. "My, Alice, are you worried about me?"

"No," she argued hotly.

If he was hurt by her answer, he didn't show it. Instead, the alien started landing soft kisses on the insides of her thighs, which made her clit throb. "If I die in battle, I asked the king to give you a choice. He can either find you a new mate, or you can be returned to Earth with your memories erased, giving you a chance to live a normal human life." His eyes softened. "Of course, your answer might change if we have babies before it happens."

Alice's throat felt tight and she wanted to change the conversation. She no longer wanted to hear about death and dying, even if she had spent the last few days angry at him. "Can we talk about something else?"

"We don't even have to talk, troublemaker."

Before she knew it, Kyvan was between her spread legs, his long, slippery, snakelike tongue caressing her sex teasingly, licking every nook and cranny of her womanhood, from her dewy petals to her tight anus.

Soft little moans escaped her mouth as her entire body trembled with each soft lick and hard thrust of his devilish tongue. Even though they had only known each other for a few weeks, it seemed Kyvan was already attuned to her body's sexual needs.

Alice let out a small scream as she reached her orgasm, her limbs flailing everywhere as she felt her wetness seep, especially on his face. Kyvan licked his lips which were shiny with her juices.

He had a silly look on his face, which only made him look more handsome. "Delicious." He grabbed a warm washcloth that he seemed to keep handy ever since he started breeding her. "Are you feeling more relaxed, little Alice?"

Alice nodded, feeling like a little fool. She should still be feeling crabby because he thought an orgasm would solve all her problems, but in all honesty, it wasn't a terrible way to spend the morning.

There was a knock on the door which caught both of them by surprise. Even though Kyvan was perfectly friendly, Alice wasn't, especially since her kidnapping, which meant he hadn't brought a lot of people over.

He tapped her knee. "Stay here."

Alice finished cleaning herself up, then she stopped short when she recognized King Korrev's voice. It was louder and less gentle than Kyvan's, which made her feel a little more sorry for Karin who she assumed was his mate.

The pair of them were speaking in hushed voices that made it hard for her to hear. Being her nosy self, Alice started tip-toeing towards the bottom of the staircase and stopping at the last two steps where the aliens wouldn't be able to see her.

Through the corner of her eye, she could see the king. He was in his human form, like Kyvan, a form both of them seemed to prefer despite their brute strength. He was wearing a pair of long leather pants, thick boots, and a long, fur-wrapped dead creature around his body, the head of the poor species wrapped around his neck.

Alice fought the urge to dry heave.

"I know you still have two months with your mate," King Korrev announced sourly, but he didn't sound very sorry at all. "But I'm here to inform you things are tense between our former allies, Yusian and Ponite. War can break out at any moment once we refuse to give them the ketenyl crystal. They haven't been keeping their end of the bargain and they have become stingy with the resources they said they would provide. You need to be ready for war at a moment's notice, even if you're busy spoiling your mate."

"I'm not spoiling her, I'm getting her to trust me, which you should try, Your Majesty."

Even though they held different positions of power, they had grown up together and Alice believed they acted like brothers.

"Is there anything else, Your Majesty?"

King Korrev cleared his throat, sounding, for the first time, a bit uncomfortable. "Yes, your mate, Allison—"

"Alice," Kyvan corrected.

"Have you managed to tame her, or do you still have to keep her tied to a leash like some of the others do, because she doesn't obey?"

Alice flinched. She knew Kyvan expected her to obey, but she had never thought the king would care too much about her obedience. *He caught you interrupting his blow job, Alice. Of course, he cares.*

"She's been more obedient," Kyvan lied for her sake. "I won't let her out until she follows my instructions and doesn't run away. Alice is well aware she won't get any privileges and a striped ass if she continues being naughty."

Alice flinched at being called naughty as if she were a toddler. She was a grown woman, for God's sake, and here he was acting like she couldn't function without his hand holding.

"Excellent, I knew you could do it. You are one of my finest warriors." Once again, the king was all business. "I would like to schedule a playdate. Will tomorrow work for you?"

Alice cocked her head to the side. A playdate? It wasn't what she had been expecting at all.

Apparently, her mate felt the same way because he was just as confused. "A playdate?"

"Yes, apparently, humans have them all the time based on my research," King Korrev continued coolly. "They use the time to play and bond. I would like you to bring Alice to a playdate with my Karin. They already met through unusual circumstances so no introductions will be necessary."

Kyvan didn't speak for a while before he reluctantly agreed. It was clear he wanted to keep her hidden away like a caged animal, but he couldn't defy the king. "All right. I will bring her after breakfast."

"Excellent." Korrev was obviously pleased. "Until tomorrow."

Alice rested her head against the wall. So, she was to have a playdate tomorrow, even if she was in her twenties. She didn't know if she wanted to be reunited with the busty blonde from a few weeks ago. Even though she was in the same boat, it was still embarrassing seeing someone so vulnerable performing sexual favors.

"You heard everything, my little eavesdropper?"

Kyvan scooped her up by picking her up around the waist as if she weighed no more than a pillow and taking her back to their bedroom again. He then tossed her on the bed, placing both hands on his hips and looking at her with disapproval.

"Are we in danger?" she blurted out. "The king said there might be an outbreak of another war and you might have to fight in it."

His face softened. "Are you worried about me, my little troublemaker?"

Alice shrugged. "Well, I don't want you to die. Not before you return me back to Earth at least."

Kyvan smiled as if she had just said a funny joke. He stroked her face. "Do not worry, little Alice. Even if a war breaks out, I am one of the king's fiercest warriors and I will persevere. You have nothing to worry about. I will make sure you are always safe."

Her heart fluttered inside her chest at his words. No man had ever cared about her safety this much. Even if he had kidnapped her, it was clear Kyvan didn't want anything bad to happen to her.

"You weren't supposed to hear that."

"King Korrev is rather loud. I couldn't ignore him if I tried."

Kyvan didn't argue with her as he pushed her down on the bed gently before grabbing her by the ankles and draping her legs over his shoulders. Her legs were spread and her ass was off the mattress.

"Don't," she whined. "I'm still sore from last night."

He raised an eyebrow. "I've licked your pussy from top to bottom. It should have helped with the soreness. Besides, I see your eyes, my little troublemaker, you're excited for this."

"I'm not," she tried to argue but scooted her butt forward.

He leaned his long neck down, to give her a slow, passionate kiss that Alice returned eagerly. Just because she was a prisoner here, didn't mean she couldn't enjoy her stay, especially since Kyvan was doing every trick under the sun to make sure she would come.

Kyvan used the opportunity when he was kissing her to part her cunt apart with his dick, which seemed to be in a perpetual state of hardness whenever she was around. Alice groaned when she felt him piercing her with his cock as he leaned forward, giving her little time to get used to his girth.

Just when Alice thought she couldn't take it anymore, he leaned forward, pushing himself a little more into her. His fingers pulled the hood hiding her clit open, exposing the little bundle of nerves which seemed to throb every time Kyvan stared at it.

Alice arched her back when he started rubbing it. The motion, combined with the way he was slowly fucking her, caused shivers to go down her spine. She twisted her body as if trying lamely to remove herself from him, but Kyvan had a firm grip on her hips.

This wasn't an erotic, fast-paced fucking like he normally gave her, where he was eager to breed her while at the same time enjoying her body. This lovemaking session felt more like a warning; he was trying his best to make it pleasurable.

"You will behave yourself at your playdate tomorrow." *Thrust.* "I don't want you being naughty like last time." *Thrust.* "You are to be pleasant with the king and Karin tomorrow even if either of them says something which displeases you." *Thrust.* "If you misbehave in any way, your little bottom hole," he circled his finger along the tight, pink muscle, "will be the one to suffer my wrath. Understood, troublemaker?"

Alice nodded, biting her lip as his thrusts became faster while he pinched her clit gently between his fingers, causing her to buck in place. "I'll be good. Please, Kyvan, let me come."

"Are you my little mate?" he asked her as he thrust one finger inside her tight anus.

"Yes," she groaned.

"Are you going to be my good girl tomorrow?" Another finger was added, spreading her muscle even more.

Alice nodded, too turned on to talk besides the occasional nod and moan. Kyvan delivered two last hard thrusts while he slapped her ass. Alice's heavy breathing could be heard as she felt his hot cum covering the backs of her thighs and seeping out of her pussy.

Alice wanted to kick herself. At the rate she was going, she was going to be pregnant with twin alien babies before the year was over. But it wasn't like she could stop Kyvan's persistent advances, especially since he was determined to breed her. If only he didn't make her feel so good, she would be able to resist a little more.

Oh, who was she kidding? An army of angry bulls wouldn't be able to stop him.

"I love you, Alice." Kyvan kissed her cheek as he rested his large frame sleepily on top of her while he ran a hand through her hair. "That's what humans say when they care for someone, right? That they love them."

Alice was too shocked to respond as the alien warrior nuzzled his face against her neck.

Chapter 8

"I'M NOT GOING without any clothes."

Kyvan sighed, obviously losing his patience as he stared at his little mate. Alice had her arms crossed over her chest which only made her breasts push forward. He was already dressed and he had even refused to leash her, another sign he was willing to trust her. Though now, in all honesty, he seemed to bitterly regret his decision.

"Females don't wear clothes, Alice, you know this. It's perfectly natural for your species to walk around naked. No harm will come to you like on Earth, especially with me here. Besides, no other mate wears clothes."

Alice gave him a dirty look, her blue eyes growing darker with rage. She did want to get out of his stuffy warrior quarters but not at the expense of her dignity. "I'm not leaving this place without clothes. I don't care if you do spank me."

Kyvan sighed as he ran a hand through his dark hair before he disappeared upstairs. Alice thought he was about to return with his famous paddle, but she was pleasantly surprised. He was holding a simple blue dress with thin straps. It was a little short for her liking, but beggars couldn't be choosers. She would just have to be careful when she bent over so she didn't flash anyone. No doubt, her alien mate would use it as an opportunity to mount her.

She touched the cotton fabric. "You got me a dress." It even matched the color of the bow around her neck. Apparently, he liked being all matchy-matchy when it came to her. Alice slipped it on, grateful at the chance to wear real clothes again. She had been naked for so long, she had forgotten what true decency and not exposing her genitals at every given moment felt like.

"I did." Kyvan stared at her, his gaze softening. "I knew you would throw a tantrum about wearing clothes sooner or later. I had them made for you since we didn't bring any female clothes over. However, when we're in private, Alice, you will remain nude. Is that understood?"

Alice nodded as she twirled around on her bare feet. It was odd how a simple dress had changed her mood so quickly. "Yes, let's go."

Kyvan offered his large hand towards her and she willingly took it, liking how rough, but warm, his hands were. Neither of them spoke as he led her towards the king's quarters which she had only seen once when she'd escaped from the healer.

The king's rooms were fancier than the quarters she and Kyvan shared and there was silver everywhere, along with massive weapons used as decorations, but also as a threat to anyone who came to visit King Korrev. He didn't seem like the type who quickly forgave those who betrayed him in any way.

Along the way, she also saw other warriors whom Kyvan greeted by nodding his head and pulling her close. The warriors barely looked in her direction. Alice guessed what Kyvan had said was true; alien warriors didn't feel attraction or desire towards human females who weren't their mates and left them alone. Even King Korrev had barely looked at her when she walked in on him naked; his entire focus had been on Karin.

Some of the warriors were alone, while others were with their mates. All of the human females were naked, like Kyvan had tried to tell her, and didn't seem the least bit embarrassed about their nakedness, unlike Alice, who blushed and tried to look away to give them privacy.

A girl with curly auburn hair waved at her, causing Alice to shyly hide behind Kyvan's arm. Back on Earth, she had never been very good at making friends. If she was to be stuck on this planet, she hoped to change that. It would be easier to start a revolution and force the stubborn alien warriors to take them back home so they could lead normal lives.

Though, much to her disappointment, all of the women seemed perfectly content and Alice was the oddball out. No wonder Kyvan was confused on why it was taking her so long to submit like everyone else. This was the first time in her academic life in which she was behind.

"Alice, you've already met Karin, correct?"

Alice shifted uncomfortably when she thought of the older woman who had been on her knees pleasuring the king with oral sex while sporting a bright red bottom. "We didn't exactly have a chance to talk. It wasn't like King Korrev let her speak. He's kind of a dictator in that way."

Kyvan nodded. "The reason the king is so strict with her is because Karin has been the hardest of the females to break. You're included in that list. Karin had been here for four months longer than you. When none of the king's warriors could tame her, he decided to take over himself. She is not the king's mate. She's his pet."

"His pet?"

Kyvan ran a hand through his dark hair. "Karin, in the

king's eyes, is not his mate. She has not earned the privilege until she submits to him completely. Therefore, until she does, she is expected to do everything the king tells her to do, no matter how outrageous the request is. He's hopeful the humiliation will break her and allow her to accept the situation she is in and no longer fight it, like she has done in the past."

"It's barbaric!" Alice spat, remembering the humiliated look on Karin's face when she had walked in on them. "He shouldn't be allowed to do that."

He shrugged. "He's the king, he is allowed to do whatever he wishes. What I'm trying to say is you need to be careful when talking to the king or Karin. I might be one of Korrev's finest warriors and childhood friend, but he does not accept betrayal well. You will also not help Karin if you try to encourage rebellion in any way, not when the king has softened towards her. He used to keep her hidden, as if he wanted to keep her all to himself. Don't ruin this for her."

Alice huffed. "You're making it seem like I have this grand plan cooked up in my head. I'm just glad to be spending time with another girl."

Kyvan curled his hand around her neck, stroking the sensitive flesh. "I am just warning you, my little trouble-maker. I know how your head works. Don't say I didn't warn you."

He knocked on the door and the bushy timke opened it by jumping on it and turning the knob to let them in. Alice smiled as she petted it on the head. The timke scowled at her before closing the door behind them. "Don't do that; it annoys them," he scolded her. "They're not like your pets back on Earth. They have a purpose."

"What's the fun in that?" she grumbled, annoyed at being scolded. He responded by slapping her on the ass, causing her to jump. Even though she was wearing a dress, it offered her very little protection, so she might as well be naked.

Alice glared at him, but he pretended not to notice as he led her towards a private garden out back. It was large and lush, filled with an arrays of trees with odd-looking flowers and fruits which were very bright in color. She was tempted to bite one of them but wasn't quite sure if they were poisonous.

The king was waiting for them impatiently, wearing similar clothes to Kyvan, but he had added a long red cape. She was glad he wasn't in his alien form. If Kyvan was scary when he wore his true form, she was positive the king looked like an absolute demon.

Karin was sitting next to him, kneeling at his feet like a perfect little mate. Alice had forgotten how beautiful she was. Back on Earth, she must have been a model of some sort. Her long, golden hair was up in two small buns while the rest cascaded down her pale shoulders.

Her lips were dark pink against her porcelain skin, and her eyes were a deep blue, completing her porcelain doll-like features. The large pink bow she wore was still tied around her slim neck, but one difference Alice noticed was her bow also included a tag with the royal symbol as well as the king's initials. Another reminder that Karin was nothing but a pet to him.

Karin was still naked as she had been when Alice had walked in on them. She was trying to shield her breasts from them, but her boobs were much larger than her own and she only managed to hide her pink-tipped nipples.

A splash of jealousy hit Alice as she looked at Kyvan to see if he was ogling Karin. She wouldn't blame him if he was; she was beautiful. Alice didn't know why she was feeling jealous of Kyvan. The man had kidnapped her, after all, and he was determined to use her as his breeding mare.

But the idea of him lusting after another woman, while he had spent the last few weeks fucking, spanking, and reassuring her how beautiful she was, rubbed her the wrong way.

However, Kyvan was barely looking in Karin's direction and, instead, seemed completely focused on the king. He had mentioned they were old childhood friends, but King Korrev was still his boss, so she guessed he couldn't be all buddy-buddy with him.

Karin had started squirming from where she was kneeling down, obviously embarrassed at the thought of having guests around to view her in this humiliating position. Alice suddenly felt guilty for being jealous of Karin. It was clear that while she was at the bottom of the totem pole, Karin was even lower.

Kyvan might be a stern disciplinarian, but he was much kinder than Korrev, who looked like he drowned puppies for fun. When he saw Karin start to squirm, he wrapped his hand tightly around her thick blonde hair, getting her attention. The blonde got the message, stiffened, and stopped squirming.

King Korrev nodded in approval as he caressed her lower chin. He then smirked at Alice when he caught her glaring at him. Only this jackass could make her go from feeling jealous to feeling sorry for the blonde. Maybe she had judged Kyvan too harshly.

The smirk Korrev had had when Alice started plotting his downfall was removed from his lips as he turned to stare at one of his oldest friends. "You're late."

"I apologize." Kyvan wrapped an arm around her waist as he pulled her close, looking slightly amused. "She insisted on a dress."

Alice blushed. He was making her seem like a toddler who had thrown a tantrum because she couldn't bring a doll to the store. She would not apologize for wanting to preserve her modesty, unlike poor Karin, whose spirit had obviously been broken by the king.

Kyvan had mentioned previously that the only reason Korrev had taken Karin in in the first place was because the other guards couldn't handle her. She would have loved to see more of Karin's fiery nature. Hell, she would help her gouge Korrev's eyes out because it was his fault both of them were in this mess.

"You're spoiling her," was all Korrev said with disgust as he tilted his strong jaw towards the garden. "You two go play. We have to talk."

"Go on, Alice." Kyvan gave her a gentle but warning push in the blonde's direction.

Karin blinked her eyes in surprise, as if she couldn't believe her good fortune that Korrev was actually letting her out from under his thumb for more than five seconds. Thankfully, the garden was huge, so both women could actually talk without worrying they would be overheard.

Kyvan had mentioned his species respected each other's mates, but Korrev seemed like the exception. The alien king seemed to have wanted to whip her ass since the first time he had laid eyes on her and there was no way in hell she was giving him the opportunity.

Karin looked a little shy as she hesitated, moving her gaze between Alice and Korrev. The jackass had no doubt broken her spirit in the short time he had decided to make her his pet. Alice scowled at Korrev, silently telling him if Kyvan would whip her ass for doing so, he would be a dead man.

The king barely blinked, probably not feeling the least bit threatened since he had bigger problems to worry about, like the invasion of neighboring planets, over a slip of a girl he could throw across the room as if she were a rag doll.

Alice took Karin to the farthest part of the garden, where

she got momentarily distracted by a purple oval fruit hanging on one of the trees.

"You can eat it," Karin said shyly when she saw Alice looking at it. "It's a bit sour, but it's good."

Alice took the fruit and ripped it in half with her bare hands. The inside was bright orange, reminding her of a sunset. She handed half of the fruit to Karin which she took gratefully. For a while, neither of them said anything as they suckled on the fruit.

"You've been here long, haven't you?" Alice finally asked once they were done. She had always been an awkward person, as her difficult life growing up wasn't exactly a conversation starter.

"Four months." Karin licked the juices off her fingers, obviously enjoying the sour fruit more than she did. Alice wondered if Korrev was starving her, but he didn't seem like the type. Like Kyvan, he seemed to rely on spanking and public humiliation over other torture methods.

Not to mention, Karin was curvy, and while she seemed generally miserable in Korrev's direction—who wouldn't be, after all—she didn't seem to be ill-treated in any form, except for her crimson cheeks.

"I came in the previous batch before you did," Karin continued.

"No one picked you?" Alice asked, genuinely surprised. Karin was a bombshell; plus, she was in her early thirties which meant she had plenty of time to pop out half a dozen babies for these caveman.

Karin touched the pink bow around her neck which, truth be told, Alice's was starting to feel like a hanging rope, especially knowing there was a tracker there. "I was very difficult when I first arrived. To the point that none of the warriors wanted me; they said I was too difficult, untamable. I made the guards' lives miserable, and the only reason they didn't kill me was because of how valuable human females are on this planet."

"Is that how you ended up as King Korrev's mate?" Alice had a sudden, new respect for the blonde. Despite her meek exterior, she seemed to have a spine.

"I'm not his mate. I'm his pet," Karin corrected flatly.

Alice winced at her poor choice of words. Kyvan had mentioned it to her, and apparently, she was a little sensitive about it. She was even lower in status than Alice, which was saying a lot since she couldn't even go to the bathroom without her mate knowing where she was.

"The only reason King Korrev took me was because none of his warriors could tame me. He told them he was going to show them how it's done. As punishment for being difficult, he made me his pet, not his queen, or even his mate. His pet. I might as well be barking for him, but he got what he wanted. He turned me into this spineless, pathetic, weepy thing with just a snap of his fingers.

Alice felt her womanhood throb with need and a little bit of curiosity. King Korrev might be a coldhearted dictator, but even she had to admit he was attractive, especially with his thick blond hair that reminded her of spun gold.

"Kyvan spanks me when I displease him." She shut her eyes. "Does Korrev do that to you too?"

Karin nodded, seemingly satisfied she was finally talking to someone who understood her woes. "He blisters my ass with whatever he can find, his hand, a switch, his belt. My butt hasn't been its original color since I stepped foot in this godforsaken place. Not to mention, I can't remember the number of times I've been on my knees sucking on his cock or having something shoved up my butt!"

Out of frustration, Karin had said the last sentence very loud. She looked over her shoulder to see if the aliens had overheard, but they seemed deep in their conversations. "I was a divorce lawyer before I was forced to be here. Do you know how embarrassing it is to be bossed around in front of everyone on a daily basis and be treated like whore?"

Alice nodded, thinking back to the many times she had found herself crying over Kyvan's lap as he whacked her bottom until he made sure sitting was not even possible in the next few days. "You were a lawyer?"

Karin puffed up her chest proudly, like an adorable flamingo, a piece of her old self peeking out. "Graduated at the top of my class from Stanford, I lived in a beautiful apartment just three blocks away from Central Park, and I had just made partner at my law firm when this happened." Her shoulders slumped in disappointment. "What about you? You look a little on the young side."

"I'm twenty-two." Alice felt hopelessly naïve standing next to a woman who obviously had her life together. "I was just about to graduate college when I was kidnapped because Kyvan took an interest in me."

Karin looked at her with pity. "Poor thing, you were just about to live your life. To think all of our accomplishments mean squat being here. We're nothing more than their baby-making machines."

Alice felt her shoulder relax. Finally, at least someone felt as frustrated as she about the prospect of being forced to deliver baby after baby. She looked over her shoulder, to make sure neither of the aliens were witnessing the change of topic in their conversation. She didn't have to be a genius to guess Korrev and Kyvan wouldn't be too happy with her if she dragged Karin into her plans. They would probably take turns spanking her.

"Listen, Karin—"

"Do you want to escape?"

Alice stared at Karin as the blonde bit her bottom lip, desperation clear in her eyes as perspiration clung to her pale skin, worried they would be found out and punished. She gulped. "Yes. But would it even be possible?"

She nodded. "Yes, I have spent the last four months waiting on that bastard hand and foot, practically glued to his side. He's the king, he has an array of visitors coming and going, he has never spared me so much as a glance when he's conversing with them." A blush coated her cheeks and Alice was suddenly thankful Kyvan had never punished her in public or made her service him when others were around.

"What do you know?"

"There are planes. Several of them. Some are only for one passengers, so those will be the ones that could make us get in and out without too much noise." She bit her pinky nail. "I doubt they will be too hard to fly. An idiot could probably do it."

Alice sucked in her breath. This was actually happening, she was near someone who knew all of the king's secrets and knew the inner workings of the palace perfectly. If anyone could get her out of here, it would be Karin.

"Where are the planes?"

"I've only been where they keep the planes once, when Korrev dragged me there when he had to inspect one of their battle planes. It's exactly twenty minutes away from here. We have to take the corridors all down the east wing until we reach the terminal. It's always busy, I doubt they will notice us."

She looked at Karin's bare breasts and curvy figure. "Maybe we should plan on hijacking some uniforms, just in case."

Karin nodded as she started squirming, obviously embarrassed of her naked form as she stared at Alice's dress with jealousy. "Perhaps you're right. It will be best." She smiled. "It's nice to have an accomplice. I must admit, back on Earth, I never did work well with people."

"Me, either. I was always a bit of a loner."

"Nothing wrong with that. The amount of people has nothing to do with the quality of them."

Happiness fluttered in her chest. For once, she was finally feeling helpful and she was glad she had someone as witty and smart as Karin on her side. She doubted she would have been able to escape by herself, no matter how much she would want to.

Besides, Kyvan had sheltered her and she didn't know the palace as well as Karin did. "When should we leave?"

"Soon." Karin lowered her voice. "Things are not so well with planets surrounding Krotev. Korrev feels there will be a war soon and he's seldom wrong about these things. When war finally starts, we shall escape. They will be too busy fighting and will hardly notice their precious mates are gone."

Karin's voice was bitter towards the end. However, Alice started feeling something else other than relief... guilt.

Despite the fact Kyvan had blistered her bottom more than once, there was something about the finality of deserting him when he was off fighting, possibly risking his life for his planet. It just felt wrong. Especially when she thought of him returning to his quarters bloody, only to find it empty.

"Alice, are you listening?" Karin looked annoyed. "I doubt the war will take long to start. A month at the most. I don't know if you noticed, but Korrev is not exactly a team player. War will happen, then we will be free. We will finally return to the lives we were meant to live, instead of just popping out babies every year. Don't you want that?"

"Of course, I do," she whispered. "It's just a little unexpected is all. Karin, but what if we're caught?"

Karin grimaced. "You'd better pray it doesn't happen; otherwise, it will be the end for both of us. Or at least for me.

Kyvan might worship you like a lovesick puppy, but there's a good chance Korrev isn't as forgiving. If we fail on this, then there is a good chance I'm dead."

Alice wiggled her bare toes on the soft grass.

Karin gripped her wrist, flashing her a fake smile. "Let's pick fruit or something. Otherwise, those two will get suspicious of why we're just standing here whispering between ourselves."

As the girls occupied themselves with picking and munching on the colorful fruit, they spoke about their old lives. Alice made Karin laugh with stories about uptight, nutty professors, while Karin shocked Alice with stories of the people she'd represented for thousands of dollars.

Before they knew it, an hour had passed and Kyvan and Korrev were approaching them. Korrev simply snapped his fingers and Karin went towards him obediently, a different picture from the headstrong woman she had just shown Alice she could be. Korrev seemed pleased with her submission as he patted her golden curls before wrapping his hand around her curvy hip. He whispered something in her ear which made Karin blush, probably something along the lines of how he was going to fuck her later since it was clear he couldn't keep his hands off her.

"Did you girls have fun?" Kyvan pressed his lips against her forehead, none the wiser.

Alice nodded.

"Wonderful, perhaps we can do this again sometime. You girls need someone to talk to, don't you? Since you're always cooped up inside." Kyvan looked at Korrev, who nodded at his request as he squeezed one of Karin's plump buttocks, not caring about them standing there.

The idea of going back to being locked inside Kyvan's quarters after discussing potential freedom with Karin, made her stomach turn. "I don't want to leave." She took a step back. This small amount of freedom had tasted too good. She had almost felt normal.

Karin shot her a warning look before Korrev pushed her head against his chest in what seemed to be a rare moment of affection. The controlling bastard was probably happy Alice was the one throwing a tantrum, and not Karin.

"Alice," he gave her a warning, his eyes glaring down on her, indicating he was close to losing his patience, "you and Karin can play another time. For now, we have to go home."

Alice knew the smart thing to do was to follow his orders, but instead, she planted her feet firmly on the ground. Perhaps it was stupidity, bravery, or her being just a brat, but she crossed her arms over her chest even though she was so insignificant standing next to him. "I'm not going. I want to stay here a little longer. Get some fresh air, which is what this human needs. Didn't your book tell you that?"

He didn't bother answering her. Instead, he scooped her up in his arms and placed her over his thick shoulder. Alice's dress rode up, exposing her bare butt. She had talked to Kyvan about adding a pair of panties, but the stubborn caveman had refused, and now she was showing her ass to Karin and Korrev.

Alice started squirming out of embarrassment, but he quickly put a stop to it by landing a hard slap on the ass cheek where his name was branded. Alice yelped as she stopped squirming. She could technically continue to try to fight him, but what was the point? The only thing she would manage to do was piss him off even more and earn herself a spanking in front of these two.

Karin winced as Kyvan hauled her ass out of there while Korrev had the audacity to wink at her. Alice pouted as she felt herself being taken out of the garden and into the familiar corridors.

His shoulder was digging into her belly and he hadn't

bothered pulling down her dress. "Can you put me down? Your shoulder is digging into my stomach."

Kyvan didn't answer, and for once, Alice didn't fight him as she let him carry her inside his quarters. Perhaps she had taken it too far, but he wasn't the one who had to be cooped up with little outside companionship for long periods of time.

He let her down once they were in their bedroom. His hands were on his thick hips as he glared down at her, making her feel smaller than she already was. "What got into you back there? You were fine this morning, and then you were acting like a complete brat."

Alice's shoulders slumped as she bit her pinky nail. "I just didn't want to leave. I was having such a fun time with Karin."

"And I promised you would see her again soon, for another playdate. You had no excuse for being stubborn and embarrassing me in front of the king. He will start thinking I have no control over you. Korrev has no patience for weak men, and just as easily as he gave you to me, he can take you away and give you to another man who is stricter than I am. Or at the very least, he will forbid you from seeing Karin because he doesn't want you to be a bad influence. Is that what you want?"

The idea of never having a female friend again made her stomach turn. Conversations with Kyvan were nice, but she was surprised to admit she missed female companionship. Not to mention, it was nice having another human to relate to.

"I never thought of it like that." She swallowed her pride. "I'm sorry."

"Good. You're about to be. I told you from the beginning, I do not tolerate disobedience. I gave you a warning not to be naughty, but you refused to follow it. Now, your ass will pay." He gripped her wrist with one hand while using his other one to reach into one of the drawers, pulling out a long, thick rope.

Perspiration clung to her forehead as she wondered what it would be used for. She didn't have to wait long, because before she knew it, she was draped over a tall, thick chair while the rope was expertly tied around her legs and arms, binding her to the piece of furniture.

Alice didn't know if she was in too much shock to fight him, or if Kyvan was just fast. She started squirming, trying to get away, even though it was impossible while her body was strapped to the chair.

The brunette flinched when she heard him unbuckle his belt. She had never been spanked with a belt before, and she almost wished he would just use his hand again. "Please," she whined as she squirmed pathetically, "I'll be good. Don't spank me."

The strong alien ignored her pathetic apologies as he pressed the belt against her behind, resting it against his name engraved on her soft skin—another way of indicating to her that he owned her. She must obey him. Kyvan was her master. Always.

"I hope you learn your lesson, Alice. This is something I do not wish to repeat."

Before she could protest again for mercy he wouldn't give her, she felt his thick, heavy belt against her sensitive nates.

Thwack!

Alice groaned as the leather dug into her pale skin a second time, then a third, and finally, a fourth, until she lost count of how many times it punished her skin. The loud slapping sound echoed in the bedroom as if mocking her punishment.

Thwack!
Thwack!

"When will you learn that you're never going to win over me, Alice?" The demon from hell she was mated to started landing the belt on the backs of her thighs, also covering them with red belt marks.

Alice yelped as she continued squirming, even though she knew it was stupid to even try, especially when he was swinging his belt.

Her cheeks bounced in the air each time the implement fell against the punished skin. Although Alice couldn't see her butt, she could explain perfectly how it looked. Red. Mottled. Covered with pink and red welts, hot enough to practically cook an egg.

"Continue being a brat all you want, Alice. It will be your ass which will pay in the end." Kyvan used his free hand to pry open her round cheeks as he landed the belt sharply against her bottom hole and her sensitive inner cheeks.

Alice could swear her cries were heard through the palace walls, even though his quarters were soundproof for this very reason. She would do everything he asked of her if he would only stop belting her.

She could feel the most sensitive parts of her inner cheeks and anus swell from the powerful strokes of the belt. Now, Alice was sore on the outside and the inside. The only thing she would be able to do for the next few days, would be to lie on her belly and think of the good ol' days when she wasn't smacked every time her alien mate saw fit.

Alice had been too busy crying, she hardly noticed when he put the belt away. Kyvan kneeled down in front of her so they were face to face. His long, pink tongue poked out of his thick lips as he started cleaning away her tears.

Her sobbing stopped when she felt his silky tongue on her face, gently caressing away the remnants of her salty tears. Alice knew she should be angry at him—he could probably use a good spitting but, instead, she was feeling oddly grateful.

She loved his gentle touches after he had properly spanked her, even if his own hands had caused her distress. Kyvan might be a strict disciplinarian, but his aftercare was phenomenal. He always tried to dry her tears and calm her down before putting her to bed. Even though the spankings were hell, Alice would always sleep like a baby after.

Kyvan licked her face for a few silent minutes until her crying had stopped. Alice stared at him with big blue eyes, wondering what he would do next. Sometimes, he would bed her, other times, he would just tuck her into bed with her bright, red rump on display.

Her hopes were on the latter; she was too sore for any lovemaking tonight.

A gentle kiss landed on her cheek, then a rougher one on her lips. "Are you going to be an obedient girl from now on, little Alice?"

Alice nodded meekly, not caring if she looked pathetic. She just wanted to be untied.

Before she could bring it up to Kyvan, he had gone behind her. At first, Alice thought she would be receiving a second dose of the spanking for not answering him, but those thoughts quickly escaped when she felt something else other than the belt.

Kyvan's tongue was on her ass.

His hot tongue, which, just minutes ago, had been wiping away her tears, was now caressing her poor, sore bottom cheeks, and it felt like it was on fire. He caressed every inch of those round, ruby cheeks, especially the multicolored welts that bloomed like a red garden, courtesy of his belt.

Alice groaned when his silky tongue passed on the welts. It still stung, but at the same time, it felt heavenly. She rubbed her thighs together as he licked her cheeks a second time.

She felt the moisture gathering between her legs as it slowly made its way down her thighs.

She gritted her teeth in confused frustration. This man/alien had just beaten her ass with a belt because she had disobeyed him, and here she was practically humping a chair because he was merely trying to make her feel better with his tongue. It was shameful. She was an embarrassment to women everywhere. She was—

Alice squeaked when she felt her sore ass cheeks being pulled apart so he could look at her bottom hole which was practically winking at him. Her entire face grew red as he leaned forward. Oh, God, why did he have to look there? It was so embarrassing.

"Your little hole is practically winking at me, troublemaker." He used his index finger to rub it in slow, teasing circles, while she tensed, waiting for him to enter a finger inside her. "It's so swollen and pink. Are you sore, little Alice?"

"Yes," she whined, practically bucking against her restraints. Her womanhood felt hot and heavy as her needy clit practically begged to be rubbed. How long was he going to torture her like this?

"Good." Kyvan landed a slap against her left butt cheek. "You deserve it for being disobedient."

Before she could whine even more, he had buried his tongue inside her ass. Every part of her bottom hole was covered with his warm saliva, reducing the achiness the belt had left behind.

Alice's legs started shaking when his tongue poked inside her tight little hole. Kyvan's fingers found her engorged clit between her swollen folds and started rubbing it in slow, circular motions as he tongue-fucked her.

Alice almost fainted when she felt his tongue enter her at the same time he rubbed the little bundle of nerves. In. Out. In. Out. Swirl.

Kyvan squeezed three violent orgasms out of her before Alice's bound body lay limp. She no longer thought about her spanked cheeks.

Kyvan landed a kiss on her sweaty forehead. "Are you going to be a good girl from now on, Alice?"

"Yes," Alice managed to pant. "I'll be your good girl."

Chapter 9

"WHAT ARE YOU LOOKING AT?"

Alice looked up at her mate, who was lying in bed after one of their lovemaking sessions two months after her first playdate with Karin. While Alice had at first worn dresses inside their home, to feel some sense of normalcy, she had quickly deserted them when Kyvan nearly tore all of them to shreds whenever he was feeling frisky enough that he decided to mount her with no prior warning. She still wore them whenever she and Kyvan ventured outside even though, as he had told her several times, no other alien would dare look at her. Some of the other mates had started teasing her because she was the only one not in the nude, but she quickly brushed them off.

As the weeks passed, Kyvan had started to trust her more and eventually even let her venture outside the palace's walls with him at her heels, as long as she continued to behave. Just last week, he had taken her to Krotev's open market, where aliens sold all kind of delicacies from different planets, including her beloved Earth, and where the population traded goods.

Kyvan had bought her a few hair ribbons and a box of her favorite cookies she had been eyeing, even though she finished half of the box in a matter of seconds. While Alice still longed for Earth sometimes, her escape plan which she had started planning with Karin during their first playdate had fallen short as she got used to life as a mate.

Alice finally got it through her thick head that she could avoid getting her butt tanned if she just followed Kyvan's directions. He was an easy man—well, half man—to please, unlike Korrev who became grouchier every time the brunette saw him. She had a feeling Korrev's relationship with the other planets' leaders wasn't going so well which was why he was in such a pissy mood.

As a result of her good girl behavior, Alice's butt had not felt a hand or an implement in two months except when Kyvan was entering her from behind when she was on all fours on the bed. Alice let it slide during those times because she enjoyed it as well.

Alice's "training time" had ended, which meant Kyvan had returned to his usual scheduled routine of protecting the king, but since he was a higher up, he was usually back in their quarters by evening.

They had settled into a routine which even Alice had no qualms about. She would usually wake up and service Kyvan with her mouth before he went to train younger warriors or discuss terribly boring things with Korrev. During the day, she would tidy up their home and entertain herself with the drawing paper and books Kyvan had bought her from the market.

Alice looked up from where she was tracing her fingers on his scar-covered chest. She didn't know why, but she liked swirling her fingers around the pink, white, and red scars, secretly imagining all of the things he had gone through.

She suddenly wondered what kind of warrior he was. He

must be good if he was the king's right-hand man. She tried to picture him as a strong, violent warrior but found out she couldn't.

Yes, he had gotten upset with her in the past, but he was never violent. In fact, he was unusually gentle compared to some of the king's other warriors.

"I'm just looking at your scars." A finger was pressed against a larger one near his clavicle. "Did they hurt?"

A twitch of a smile appeared on his face. "What do you think?" He reached for her hand, landing kisses on each of her fingers. "Thankfully, we have good healers and I'm made of sterner stuff."

"Do you cry when you're hurt?" Alice remembered when she had broken her foot in the fifth grade and she had cried buckets.

Kyvan looked at her as if she were nuts. "Of course not. When you're in the heat of battle, you hardly notice the pain. Your only thoughts are to get out alive."

Alice sat up. "Did you always know you wanted to be a warrior? Wasn't there anything else you wanted to do?" Even though she asked him that, she couldn't imagine him working at the market or owning his own shop. He would probably get bored easily.

"It's not what I wanted, it is what is expected. My father was a warrior who served the previous king, and it was expected I would also be a warrior. Just like Korrev knew he was always destined to be king when his father died." Kyvan looked at her frowning face. "It's not a death sentence, little Alice. It is what we are made to do. We've been preparing for this moment since we were children. I, training to be a warrior, and Korrev, training to be king."

Alice frowned. "That doesn't sound like much of a childhood."

"When we were growing up, there was hardly a moment

of peace." He placed a hand on her flat belly. "Do not worry. When our children are born, I will make sure they enjoy their childhood as much as possible before they are expected to become warriors."

Alice wrinkled her nose as she pulled away. "What's with your obsession with knocking me up?"

Kyvan chuckled as he nuzzled his head against her dark hair. "Like I said, I have my destiny, and you have yours."

Their lovey-dovey conversation was interrupted when there was a knock on the door. He gave her a warning look. "Stay. I'll be right back." He quickly got dressed in a pair of blue trousers. "Don't eavesdrop, brat, like you normally do."

Alice gave him a cheeky smile, not promising anything. He responded by giving her a sharp smack on her rump.

Even though she knew she would more than likely get a whipping for it, Alice found herself tiptoeing to the bottom of the staircase. Thankfully, there was a large wall she could hide behind to shield herself.

She recognized Korrev's stern voice almost immediately even though he was trying and failing to lower his voice, possibly to her mate's request.

"We have tried and failed to reach a peaceful agreement. A battle is happening, whether you like it or not. What has caused you to become so soft?" Korrev raised an eyebrow in a mocking tone, making Alice want to slap the smile off his face. "Is it perhaps your bratty little mate who has made you forget you are a warrior first?"

Kyvan gritted his teeth. "As if you're not the same for Karin. We both have someone who needs us now. We can't simply go into battle as if nothing has changed."

"We cannot let ourselves be annihilated, either, because we want to protect them. Consider this your only warning, Kyvan. When the fight begins, you must be ready." His words were cold and uncaring even when mentioning Karin. He must care for her in his frigid, heartless way.

"I understand." Even though his words were respectful, she had a feeling Kyvan wanted to slap him silly.

"I'm putting Karin in a cage when the battle begins. She will be safely guarded. I have an extra cage if you wish."

Alice balked at being put into a cage like a rabid animal. No wonder Karin despised him.

"Thank you for the offer, but I will not be putting Alice in a cage. She has been behaving extremely well these past two months. She has my full confidence."

Alice's heart fluttered at Kyvan's words, but she also couldn't help but feel a bit guilty that at some point, she had been planning on running away with Karin. She dug her nails in her thigh. She wasn't even sure if that was what she wanted anymore.

Korrev snorted but didn't argue with him as he shut the door behind himself.

Alice was so busy with her own thoughts that she hardly noticed when Kyvan towered over her. "Alice, what are you doing here?"

Alice looked at him with big, blue eyes. "Are you going to be okay? I mean, are you going to die?"

He sighed as he picked her up and placed her over his shoulder, carrying her back upstairs, a pose she was all too familiar with. Once they were back in the bedroom, he placed her on the bed, kneeling in front of her.

His fingers were pressed underneath her chin, forcing her to look at him. "Listen, you have nothing to worry about. Korrev likes to be dramatic sometimes."

"Are you going to put me in a cage like Karin?"

"No. Do you want me to? You two could keep each other company."

As much as she liked Karin, she didn't fancy being in a cage. It would just make her feel claustrophobic.

"No, I would rather stay here. I promise I'll behave."

"Good girl."

"Kyvan?"

"Yes?"

"Will you train me?"

He blinked. "Train you?"

"Yes," she bit on her pinky nail, "to defend myself, just in case something happens. I know you want to protect me, but I want to protect myself too."

Kyvan looked doubtful. Clearly, he wanted to keep her in a pretty glass cage like the king was doing to Karin. But Alice couldn't do that. She felt something restless in her belly, like she should be ready, in case anything came her way, like large enemy aliens who could probably stomp her like a bug if they wanted to.

He must have noticed her determination because he slowly nodded. "All right. We can do some training this after-noon. A few basics wouldn't harm anyone. The minute it becomes too much, you must tell me. Is that understood, Alice?"

Alice nodded eagerly.

Later that afternoon, after lunch, Alice found herself in one of Kyvan's training rooms that the other warriors used for practice. It was a large, airy room at the end of the palace, filled with all kinds of weights and weapons that she had no idea what they were used for.

Alice picked up a large, heavy spear with what seemed like colorful rocks attached to it. It was heavy, but she managed to carry it. "What is this? Can we try practicing with this first?"

Kyvan glared at her before slapping her on the butt, causing her to squeal. "Don't touch it. You'll blow your foolish head off." He reached into his pockets and pulled out a small dagger. "Here, you'll use this."

She looked at it, wrinkling her nose. "It's too small and pathetic."

"You will use it, and you will like it, or I shall take Korrev's offer into consideration and lock you in with Karin if you can't listen to directions.

Alice grumbled something about unfairness under her breath but took the dagger. Kyvan then gave her a boring speech about protecting her face and her chest which she hardly listened to.

Once he was done, he stared down at her. "Attack me."

Alice looked at the mountain of a man. "Attack you, but—"

"You won't hurt me."

"I'm actually afraid you'll hurt *me*."

He rolled his eyes. "I would never hurt you. Now, either attack me, or let's go."

Alice hesitated before she leaped forward like a bunny, aiming for his neck. Kyvan managed to throw her on the floor, somehow being gentle about it. He had barely moved his hand, as if she was an annoying fly.

"Again. Try using the dagger this time."

Alice nodded as, this time, she tried attacking him from the side with sheer determination. Surely, she would be able to make it, she just knew if— Alice's thoughts were interrupted when her hand was twisted so the dagger fell on the floor.

She glared at him. "That was a cheap shot!"

"How so?" Kyvan let go of her arm. "You left yourself wide open. Not to mention, you are incredibly slow."

"Have you forgotten I'm human? Not all of us have sonic speed."

"Which means there is less of a chance they will go easy

on you. They will see you as an easy target." Kyvan removed the dagger from her. "Let's work on the fundamentals first, getting away in case you are taken."

Kyvan wrapped his strong arms around her, causing a delicious shiver to go down her spine. She clenched her pussy. Dammit, she should not be feeling turned on right now. He rested his chin on her shoulder. "Now, let's say someone wraps his arms around you from behind. What should you do?"

"Scream?" she joked.

He ignored her as he pointed to her elbow. "This can be one of your strongest weapons. Jam your elbow against the attacker's stomach several times, as hard as you can. Eventually, it will trigger a reaction, allowing you to escape. Do not stay and fight, Alice; you must work on finding yourself a hiding place. Is that understood?"

She nodded as she blushed when his lips brushed against her ear. "Let's try it."

The day after her training, every muscle in Alice's body felt like it was on fire. She could barely take two steps without bursting into tears, even though Kyvan had gone easy on her. By their stopping point the day before, Alice still wasn't very good, but at least she could defend herself somewhat.

Kyvan tried to reassure her they would never go after her. He would, as he had told her at least a dozen times, keep her safe. But she couldn't ignore the fear in her belly, either. This was the first time she had ever been in danger of being potentially attacked. Back on Earth, she was a nobody. Here, she was Kyvan's mate and, therefore, an easy target.

Alice was currently lying down on her belly, resting after Kyvan had put some type of green goo over every inch of her body, including her ass which he claimed would help with the achiness she was feeling.

She was too tired to realize this was the first time he had

left her alone for longer than five minutes. Probably because he realized she couldn't move faster than a snail's pace.

Alice bit her lower lip as she snuggled against the pillows, wondering if Korrev was right and they would unleash into a never-ending war against enemy planets. If Kyvan died, what would happen to her?

Three months ago, she would have been over the moon at the mention of a dead Kyvan, but if the universe would ask her right now, she wouldn't be sure what her answer would be. Yes, he was a brute with a heavy hand who couldn't care less about her tears when he was blistering her ass, but he was still kind in his own alien warrior way. He would kiss her sweetly every chance he got, buy her treats from the market even when she was acting like a spoiled brat, and when he was making love to her, he would always make sure she orgasmed first.

The idea of a dead Kyvan, made her shudder with dread. What would she do if she never saw him smiling again or if she never felt his firm body under her? Would she even want anyone else? Had he ruined men for her?

She knew he had promised she would have a choice if worse came to worse, either returning to Earth with her memories erased, or staying in Krotev with another mate. But she didn't want another mate; she wanted Kyvan. For all she knew, the jackass King Korrev would just take her with him so Alice and Karin would form some kind of perverted harem for the bastard.

Her depressing thoughts were interrupted when the door opened. Alice quickly raised her head even though she winced at the pain.

Kyvan was carrying some kind of box in his hands. He shook his head at her pathetic stance. "Are you still in pain? We barely practiced for two hours and it wasn't intense at all."

"Not everyone has a six pack," she snapped. Her new life was more sedentary, with the exception of their lovemaking. As a result, she had grown softer and rounder which she was self-conscious about, but apparently, her alien mate seemed to love. "What's in the box?"

"I'm not going to tell you if you're in a crabby mood."

Alice sucked in her cheeks. "Fine. I promise I'll behave."

"Good girl." He placed the box down and opened it slowly. When she saw what was inside, Alice screamed while Kyvan simply looked confused. "What is it?"

"What is that?" she shrieked, hiding behind the couch. "Take it away! Or better yet, kill it!"

"Why would I do that? It was terribly expensive. I thought it would make you happy, troublemaker."

"Why would it make me happy?"

"Because it's a present for you."

While Alice loved presents, she wasn't particularly fond of the one he had just presented for her inspection. The creature in the box was tiny, bright yellow, and fuzzy like a carpet. It was also cute in a weird, horror movie sort of way, with large antennas above its large black eyes. Its body was short and fat, sprouting a long tail which divided itself into four smaller ones.

The creature blinked back at her as it was wondering what she was hollering about.

Alice gulped. "What is it?"

"It's a lemex." He scooped it up and started walking to her. "They're quite rare and expensive. Lemexes are only found in a specific part in Krotev and they're very hard to catch. The late king, Korrev's father, was quite fond of them. I thought you would be too. I even bought you a female one because you're always complaining you're tired of being the only girl around. Don't worry; she won't bite. She is quite docile. They had different colors at the market, and I was looking for blue, to match your bow, but I had to settle for yellow."

"I like yellow," she whispered. Her hand reached towards the creature, then she rested it on her head. The lemex looked confused, before she licked her hand. Like Kyvan, in his alien form, she also had a long, pink tongue. The dark eyes were a bit creepy, though, but she supposed she could ignore them, given how much trouble he went through.

She let out a nervous giggle. "It's kind of cute. Like a cat or a dog."

"These are more useful. They can jump fifty feet into the air, and when they are feeling threatened, their fangs are poisonous," he announced proudly.

The lemex seemed to grin at her as she showed her pointy fangs. She made a mental note never to anger it. "She's kind of cute. It will be nice not to be alone in the house all the time. Thank you. I appreciate it."

Kyvan looked pleased as he kissed her. "She'll need a name."

The bright yellow color reminded her of a newborn chick. "Chicky."

Chapter 10

BOOM!

Alice's eyes flew open the moment she heard the terrible sound and the palace walls started shaking. Kyvan was up and dressing in his warrior gear before she could even sit up and question what the hell was going on.

She jumped out of the bed, running towards the window, with Chicky hot on her heels hissing at her ankles. Even she felt the danger.

Alice's blue eyes narrowed as she glanced at the sky. Dark. Ominous. There were gold-colored spaceships falling from the sky. Alice didn't even want to think about what type of creatures were on them.

A strong hand gripped her shoulder before pulling her away. She stared at Kyvan, for the first time noticing something new crossing his features. Fear.

"Get away from the window," he said to her, not his usual loving self. A loud bell could be heard all over the palace, as warriors shuffled out of their quarters, carrying weapons and yelling out orders. "Alice, I have to go, Korrev needs me. You must promise me you will stay here with Chicky. Don't move." He forced the dagger into her hand. "Don't make me regret not locking you in a cage."

"But what if they come here?" she blurted out.

"They won't. They want to lure us out. The palace has too many weapons. Now, remember, stay." He pulled her into his arms, giving her a deep, aggressive kiss. Alice savored it, her pessimistic mind thinking the worst. "I'll be back before you know it."

Alice bit her lower lip. "You won't die?"

"I have fought and survived many battles, little Alice. This is no different. Korrev and I will not stop until we have our enemies on their knees." With that last statement, he gave her another kiss before he departed the quarters.

Alice sighed as she sat on the bed while Chicky rubbed her yellow fur against her legs, her fangs sharp and wide as red poison dripped from her teeth, ready to attack the first enemy who came through those doors. But no one came.

Every minute that ticked by felt like hell to Alice, like the universe was mocking her. First, she had been kidnapped by an alien she couldn't stand, and the second he was starting to be the least bit tolerable, there was a huge risk of him not coming back.

She shut her eyes, hearing the explosions, war cries, and the sounds of weapons flying by beside her. Alice tapped her foot nervously until Chicky hissed at her, obviously annoyed. Her hand gripped the dagger.

Alice stood up. Kyvan was going to kill her, but she couldn't just sit there without doing anything. Alice wasn't quite sure what she was going to do once she reached the battlefield, but it was better than just waiting like a moron.

Chicky whined, begging her to take her with her. "Sorry, Chicky." She patted the alien's head. "You stay here and guard the place." Chicky glared, showing off her tongue.

Alice left her behind, holding the dagger tightly in her

hand, wishing desperately she had shoes, but she hardly needed them because she spent ninety percent of her time in the palace. At least she had her dress and didn't have to be nude.

The girl didn't know where she was going, since she didn't even have a plan. She just went to where she heard the explosions and the screams.

Alice's legs ran fast along the corridors. She realized how surprisingly easy it was to navigate through the palace without guards at every corner. Before she knew it, she was touching outside soil.

Kyvan was right. They didn't fight in the palace, but they weren't far off, either. The scene in front of her felt like it was out of a movie. Alice stood frozen, not sure what to do or where to move. All she knew was she needed to find Kyvan.

The place where the fighting was occurring was a few feet away from the palace where, usually, the market was held daily. Except, the once beautiful courtyard was destroyed, the only thing remaining was gravel and pieces of torn buildings, bits of armor, and fallen weapons.

Alice recognized the graceful, large bodies of the Krotev warriors fighting two different groups of aliens. One of them consisted of large, green creatures with broad shoulders, bulging eyes, and large ram-like horns poking out from the sides of their heads. The other group consisted of slightly smaller purple aliens, with three arms on each side and a large eyeball in the center of their faces.

Alice shivered; maybe the Krotev aliens weren't too bad looking after all.

The fighting was brutal. Different colored blood was spilled everywhere and it was clear each group was determined to inflict as much damage as possible. Alice found herself wincing at the way they easily swung their weapons around, secretly wondering why Kyvan found fighting so fascinating while she thought it was stomach churning.

Her blue eyes scanned the fighting taking place. Perhaps she should have listened to Kyvan and just stayed in the palace. There were no other mates here, only her stupid ass.

She saw King Korrev at the far back, fighting one of the green aliens with what looked like a large ax almost gracefully. While she recognized some of the other warriors, she didn't see Kyvan anywhere.

Alice felt herself being picked up from behind and dangled in the air like a fish out of water by one of the purple aliens with the freakishly large amount of arms. He grinned at her and Alice counted no less than forty-two teeth.

"What is this?" he questioned as he squeezed her waist. "Supper? So tender."

Before her nerves got the best of her, Alice found herself raising the dagger she held in her hand, digging it into the one eyeball. The alien screamed as stinky green pus began to ooze out of the eyeball.

Alice moaned when she was unceremoniously dropped on the ground, the sharp gravel digging against her face and body.

"Alice!" Kyvan barked from behind her. "What are you doing here? I told you to stay inside. You never listen."

Alice's heart jumped in her chest when she recognized his angry voice, which usually meant she was just seconds away from being punished. But this time, she didn't care. Kyvan was okay. He was here in front of her.

He was pissed off, exhausted, and his gear was covered in bodily fluids, but he was alive. "Come here!" he ordered.

Alice happily did as she was told, nearly skipping with glee. He was alive; he was well. They would be together soon.

Alice ran to him, reaching her arm forward so she could grip his hand. His fingertips were just out of reach when she felt a sharp pain sprouting out of her midsection. With wide eyes, she looked down. Her stomach region was covered with blood, a sharp, heavy sword poked out of it.

Her legs trembled; it was as if her mind couldn't comprehend what she was seeing. A sword was actually poking out of her. It felt heavy. The weapon probably weighed as much as she did.

She felt something heavy rise up in her throat before blood covered the ground as she vomited the heavy liquid all over herself. Alice closed her eyes. She had never vomited blood before. Alice could safely say it was not a pleasant experience.

"Alice!" Kyvan roared, pointing his own sword at the alien who had stabbed her.

Alice's legs shook as the sword was removed from her. A whimper escaped her lips as she felt herself fall to the ground headfirst. The pain was slowly disappearing except for a light throbbing, and if binge watching medical shows taught her anything, it was that once she stopped feeling pain, it meant she was close to the end.

Did this mean she was going to die?

Dammit. This had not been how she wanted to die, a bloody, ugly mess.

You never told Kyvan you loved him, dummy, she scolded herself, her vision becoming blurry from the lack of blood. *He told you he loved you, but you never had the guts to tell him how much you loved him. Coward. Now you'll die and he will never find out.*

"Alice! Alice, look at me." Kyvan gently turned her to her side. He had a crazy, vengeful look in his eyes as he cradled her head gently in his hands. His face was covered with a purple liquid which she guessed was the other alien's blood.

"K-Kyvan." She shut her eyes tightly. "Hurt."

"I know, baby," he choked out as he started caressing her face, trying to wipe away the blood. "Don't worry. Azis will be here soon. He'll patch you up, but you'll need to stay with me, Alice. Do not fall asleep."

"Tired." She protested as she gripped his gear. Her eyes were drooping, her tongue heavy. She could barely form coherent sentences even though he kept calling her name. "I- I l-love you."

Chapter 11

"YOU CANNOT SEE HER."

Azis didn't flinch when Kyvan slammed his fist against the wall, breaking through the hard concrete. His body was covered with the blood of his enemies, his face and arms covered with bruises and additional marks. However, he felt no pain at all, only a mixture of worry and anger.

Worry plagued his whole body because of his injured little sweetheart whom he had immediately taken to the healer, only to return to the battle scene to slaughter everyone in his sight. It had impressed Korrev enough that he had made him second in command on the spot, but he didn't care about the honor, he just wanted Alice.

This bastard Azis wasn't letting him see her and if he wasn't a damn good healer, he would have strangled him on the spot.

"Why not?" he demanded, his voice harsh. Each word was cold and unforgiving.

"Because I just finished her surgery and she needs rest." Azis didn't look fazed at all by his screaming. "She has thirty-two stitches holding her belly together, thanks to the poisonous sword. She should consider herself lucky her foolish self is still alive. Why was she there? Why didn't you put her in a cage?"

He ignored the question as he stepped forward. "Let me see her. Now."

Azis probably knew he was seconds away from being punched, because he stepped aside. "Cot seven. Five minutes. She needs rest. She might not make much sense, the painkillers I gave her are strong. Is the fighting over?"

"Yes. They surrendered as they were going to. The king is talking to them now." Kyvan's murder spree had certainly helped speed up the process. Kyvan went to cot seven, where he found Alice sleeping. Her dress had been torn off and she was nude. Long, thick bandages were wrapped around her stomach tightly. Her face was pale and even though she was asleep, her facial features were twisted in pain.

"Alice." Kyvan kneeled down next to next, clutching her hand. "Talk to me. I need to hear your voice, sweetheart."

Alice stirred a little in her sleep.

"Alice, say something. Anything, then you can sleep. Please, baby."

"K-Kvyan." She stirred a bit, her blue eyes opening. She winced, obviously still in pain. "Hurt."

"I know, baby." Kyvan kissed her forehead. "How are you feeling? They had to place special stitches in your belly to sew it back together so it would heal properly. The sword was poisonous."

"I'm fine," she squeaked, which was clearly a lie. She had always been a terrible liar, which he thought was adorable.

"You have thirty-two stitches inside your weak, delicate human body. How 'fine' could you possibly be?" He pressed a hand gently against her cheek, growling. "Why did you do such a foolish thing such as coming after me in the middle of a battle?"

"I wanted to see you," she reassured him weakly. "I-I just couldn't stay inside. I was afraid I would never see you again."

"You're such a little fool." Kyvan snapped, but there was no malice in his voice, only resignation. "If you ever do something which gets you hurt again, Alice, I will blister your ass every day for a month. Understood?"

She nodded, but she was only half listening, her eyes drooping.

Kyvan sighed as he kissed her. "Sleep, sweetheart. I'll be here when you wake up, even if I have to kick Azis out."

Alice sighed, closing her eyes. "Kyvan?"

"Yes?"

"I love you." Her eyes watered with emotion. "I'm sorry I didn't tell you before, but I love you so much."

"I know." He kissed her again, squeezing her cheek gently. "I love you too. Very much."

"How could you tell what I was feeling?"

"Because I saw the way you looked at me."

"Please, please." Just three weeks after the operation which had saved her life and where Azis had basically stitched her stomach back together as if she were a rag doll, Alice was humping her mate's legs. Given the way Kyvan was glaring at her, it was clear he did not appreciate being fondled even though he had done the same to Alice since she had stepped foot on Krotev. "Please, Kyvan, I need it."

The pain in her belly had mostly disappeared, thanks to the heavy painkillers Azis had prescribed her, though he had mentioned it would be at least three more months before her special stitches would be able to be removed. The sword had been poisonous and had caused enough damage to her stomach that Azis had to sew it together piece by piece, something he liked to annoyingly remind her of every time Kyvan took her to her biweekly checkup.

Since she was feeling better and her belly was healing nicely, thanks to the stitches Azis had provided, the healer had given his approval for them to have sex again, though he had warned them that any spanking or sexual activity should be done in a very gentle manner.

Unfortunately for her, this was one of the few times Kyvan seemed to have no interest in sleeping with her which was, quite frankly, driving her mad.

Her hand went towards his crotch which he very easily slapped away sharply. Alice whimpered, "Please don't torture me. I know you're still mad that I didn't follow your directions, but I am so horny right now. You have no idea how painful it is."

Kyvan sucked in his breath, but she could see he was getting rock hard. The shorts he was wearing barely hid his bulge. "And I told you no, Alice. Not until Azis removes every last stitch from your belly."

"But that could take months!"

"Then you should have thought of the consequences before you ran into the battlefield."

Alice's bottom lip trembled. "But I was coming to see you. I was worried about you. You can't punish me for loving you."

Kyvan sighed, obviously torn by her trembling. "Now, don't start crying because I'm holding you accountable for your actions." He paused, his eyes darkening. "If we are doing this, Alice, we are doing it my way. Is that understood?"

Alice nodded, her eyes shining; she could practically feel herself getting wet with anticipation.

"Sit up. Spread your legs. Play with your breasts," he

ordered gruffly as he watched the brunette open her legs, exposing her wet slit. Her hands were immediately on her breasts, alternating between squeezing them and twisting her nipples, making them a dark berry color.

Kyvan licked his lips as he watched Alice play with herself, thrusting her eager little hips into the empty air. He could feel himself growing harder, the more he watched her growing wetter by him watching her.

"Now use one hand to touch yourself between your legs. Spread your lips and rub your little clit." The girl whimpered, but she was surprisingly obedient today as one of her hands disappeared between her legs, while the other continued caressing her boobs.

Up. Down. Clockwise. Counterclockwise.

Alice's legs bucked as she pleasured herself. She could feel her wetness dripping from her body as she touched herself, and Kyvan's dark eyes narrowing on her sex wasn't helping. It was just making her more wet.

The throbbing between her legs intensified, as if it were begging for his manhood. Her cheeks were flushed bright red as she looked at him with pleading eyes. "Kyvan, please, I can't take it anymore."

He smirked, not moving an inch. "Now you know half of the desperation I felt when I saw you in the bed fighting for your life."

"Please, please make me come. I'm sorry. I'll be a good girl. I swear. Just please take this ache away."

Kyvan gripped her by the waist, flipping her over gently until she was in the familiar position, on all fours. "Spread your cheeks," he ordered. "Press your body against the mattress. I want your tight little butt in the air. Now, Alice."

Alice hesitated a bit, but then did as she was told.

She felt very vulnerable as she lay there with her spread ass in the air, her pucker twitching against his stern glare.

Several moans escaped her as his hot tongue started caressing every nook and cranny of her pink bottom hole, covering it with his saliva.

It felt so good. So slippery. So warm. So erotic.

Alice would never have tried it with another man, but with Kyvan, it felt just right. She held in her breath as she felt Kyvan slip one finger inside her, then two stretching her as far apart as he could once she was properly lubed up.

"I'm going to put my cock up your tight little ass, Alice," he whispered in her ear. "That should remind you, next time, to think before you act. Is that understood?"

Alice whimpered as she slowly nodded while he thrust both thick fingers in and out of her ass. "Oh, Kyvan, I will do whatever you want, just please fuck my ass."

He smirked. "Oh, troublemaker, you might come to regret those words."

Kyvan's fingers were removed from her ass, only to be replaced by his stiff shaft which entered her little by little, spreading her tight little hole open. Alice yelped when he got his cock halfway in her tight, virgin hole.

Her fingers gripped the sheets, but even if she attempted to pull away, he had a tight grip on her hips. Kyvan's gentleness ended right then and there as he pushed his complete length inside her, introducing her to a feeling of fullness she had never felt before.

Alice's rosebud throbbed as it struggled to accept all of him even with how wet her backside was. Her sphincter felt incredibly sore, the more he forced himself in, to the point she was almost afraid he was going to tear her in two.

Her fingers gripped the bedspread as he continued fucking her slowly, letting her get used to every inch of him. His rough fingers found her weepy clit and he started rubbing her needy clit with each thrust.

Alice felt a rush of different emotions the more attention

her lower body received. But all of them were good. Love. Desire. Fullness.

She had always been a little nervous when it came to anal sex, even before she had been transported to Krotev, but she was surprised to admit she enjoyed it. Alice was sure it was because she was experiencing it with her mate whom she knew would never hurt her.

"You are to never disobey me again, Alice, is that understood?" he growled as he slapped her ass, decorating it with a pale pink handprint. "From now on, you will be my good girl, understand?"

Alice responded with a scream as he came inside her, filling her with his warm, salty seed. He pulled out of her slowly, making a low, wet, erotic sound as his cock left her tight hole.

Alice let out a low moan as she planted herself into the mattress, her face hot as she felt his hot seed leaking from between her cheeks. Kyvan immediately looked alarmed. "Alice, what's wrong? Are you okay? Was I too rough?"

She gave him a sleepy smile. "You were just perfect."

Kyvan kissed her forehead. "Are you sure you're not in pain?"

"I'm just a little sore," she admitted as she started caressing his face. "But I'm sure I will be all right. I did survive a sword stabbing me in the stomach."

Kyvan glared at her, obviously wanting to scold her, but then his features relaxed as one thumb caressed the surgical scar on her belly. "I love you, my little Alice."

Alice took his hand, kissing his knuckles. "I love you more."

Chapter 12

FOUR MONTHS LATER...

When Kyvan and Azis finally declared her healthy enough to return to normal activities after the stitches in her stomach had been removed, the first thing Alice did was request a playdate with Karin.

It had taken longer than she had anticipated because Kyvan was being dramatically overprotective and wanted to keep her all to himself after he had nearly lost her. She had spent more time with his cock buried between her legs than standing. Korrev, on the other hand, had no excuse, he was just being his usual asshole self who didn't let Karin have any fun. Though he seemed to have grown softer on her since the battle ended. At least her butt wasn't always red anymore.

Alice had asked Karin if she had seen any of the battle, but she had responded glumly that the king had kept her in a cage with two of his guards keeping watch on her, even though they would rather have been fighting than babysitting her.

They were back in the garden where they had been during their first playdate. Korrev and Kyvan whispered among themselves in secret at the front of the garden while the girls were in the back.

The playdate wasn't going as Alice had hoped. Karin was unusually quiet. She wondered if the blonde and the king were having problems as the pair had seemed distant when he had greeted Alice and Kyvan. She had noticed the cold-ness in his voice when he had instructed her, "Go play with Alice, Karin."

It had been four months since Alice had seen the blonde, and she couldn't believe the vast changes in her. She had lost a large amount of weight, her breasts didn't seem as big and she could see her ribs poking out. Her blonde hair wasn't as shiny while dark circles adorned her eyes.

"Are you okay?" Alice asked as they sat down on the green and blue picnic blanket she had sewn. She had been feeling unusually domestic and had been sewing a lot more lately. Kyvan had even bought her materials, happy she was keeping herself occupied instead of becoming a walking target. "You look tired. Are you sick?"

"No." Karin pressed a hand against her bare knee. "I'm just sad. I thought by now I would be back in New York. Not still here."

"Is Korrev still being an asshole?"

"He's been busy lately, so he doesn't even have time to be an asshole," she admitted glumly. "But at least my butt is getting some rest. Korrev is not the problem, at least not entirely. I just hate being here because I'm bored. Back in New York, I was always so busy with one case or another that I hardly slept. Here, I have nothing to look forward to except playdates with you and…" She flushed but didn't finish her sentence, probably about to say the only good thing about being with Korrev was the sex. "I keep telling Korrev I'm bored, but his response is just to tire me out with sex. I guess not even alien men listen."

"Give him time," Alice insisted, even though she knew her advice was less than helpful and borderline useless. "Things are just returning to normal. The palace is large, I'm sure the king will find you something to do."

"The war has been over for months," Karin announced bitterly. "You and I both know Korrev is a controlling nutcase who will not let me out of his sight. I made my decision. I'm going to leave, Alice. I've managed to steal one of the uniforms the aliens wear when they are fixing the planes so their bodies are protected. I'm just looking for the perfect opening which will allow me to go."

Alice didn't say anything. She thought back to when they had first made the plan. It sounded childish to her now. "Korrev will make your life miserable if you're caught."

Karin gave a bitter laugh. "Let him, he cannot make me more miserable than I am now." She looked at her wearily. "I suppose this is your way of saying you no longer want to come with me."

Alice patted her hand. "No, I'm sorry. I know I agreed with you at the beginning, but I have decided to stay. I don't quite understand it myself, yet I suppose people rarely understand love, but I love Kyvan. After the months we have spent together I cannot imagine leaving his side, ever. I'm sorry, Karin, I will not go with you. However, I will wish you the best. I hope you return to the world you miss. I know you have everything figured out, but let me give you some advice. Please make sure you think things through thoroughly, because once you go through with it, there is no turning back."

Karin nodded, the color once again leaving her face. Korrev must have noticed because he gave them a hawklike stare before she reassured him they were fine.

"I might not be able to say goodbye to you before I leave."

"I understand. I hope you make it, Kar."

"Thank you, Alice. Thank you for being my friend during my time here. You made it seem not as lonely."

Alice cleared her throat. "Korrev arranged the first play-date, actually. He told Kyvan he was afraid you were lonely and arranged the whole thing."

Karin looked surprised. "He did? He told me Kyvan was worried about you being lonely."

"Please, Kyvan and I were at each other's throats the first few days, so I had no time to feel lonely. I know Korrev is an asshole, but he does care about you in his own selfish way. He could have killed you for being a headache to the guards at the beginning, but he didn't."

"Perhaps he is more perceptive than he lets on," Karin murmured. "But still, it doesn't make him a saint. Your Kyvan is different, though, he might be a caveman, but he's still loving. Almost like a regular human male, with double the testosterone, that is."

"Well, he's been obsessed since the beginning, so I think it helps. Besides, as far as warriors go, Korrev thinks he's tenderhearted."

Karin snorted, but she looked slightly amused. "Korrev thinks anyone who is against decapitation is tenderhearted."

"Time to go, little Alice."

Alice looked up to see Kyvan staring down at her before wrapping an arm gently around her waist, scooping her up. She rolled her eyes. It had been four months since she had been injured and he still insisted on treating her like a puppy with a broken leg.

She said her embarrassing goodbyes to Karin and Korrev before they headed back to their quarters, with him still carrying her like a sack of flour.

"Is everything okay with Karin? She looked a bit peaked."

Alice didn't know if he was suspicious or not. "She's fine, just tired. Your king is a headcase after all."

Thankfully, Kyvan didn't question her anymore.

"I told you, I'm fine. I don't need to see a healer," Alice grumbled as she squirmed, trying to get away, but it was hard to do when Kyvan's broad shoulder was digging into her belly as he carried her to Azis' clinic. "I'm fine, now put me down."

"You've lost weight."

"I've always been scrawny."

"You haven't been sleeping."

"It's hard to do when you insist on hugging me all night."

"You haven't been eating much, either."

"I think Krotev needs to open more fast-food joints."

"You've been nauseous."

"Because you keep being a pain in my ass," Alice grumbled under her breath as Kyvan slapped her ass in response. "I was kidding!"

They entered Azis' nearly freezing clinic as the elderly alien waited from them, obviously impatient. "At least you got that ridiculous dress off her," he said as a form of greeting as he placed her on all fours as if she were nothing more than a rag doll.

She looked at Kyvan nervously, but the alien simply patted her head. "Be good, Alice. I'll give you a treat and then we'll spend the afternoon with Chicky, how does that sound?"

Before she could respond, Alice found herself being prodded by Azis' thick figures in her womanhood as he grumbled complaints underneath his breath. It was hard not to resent him when he was treating her like cattle, but at least he wasn't a pervert, so that was a plus.

Azis fondled her for a few more silent minutes, mainly her nether regions, but also her bottom and breasts. Then he entered what seemed and felt like a long, thick dildo inside her which felt warm, causing a tickling sensation. The healer did not seem to appreciate her fit of laughter, but at least Kyvan found it cute.

After what seemed like hours, he pulled back, satisfied. "Congratulations, Kyvan. Your mate is with child. Three months pregnant if I'm not mistaken. You shall have your son in your arms before you know it. Congratulations, again, as I know Alice is a headache."

Alice glared at him, his rudeness overshadowing the fact she had been bred successfully. Her thoughts returned to her upcoming pregnancy when her mate picked her up in his arms, pressing her to his chest before engulfing her in a deep kiss.

"Did you hear, Alice? We're going to have a baby!" Before she could even utter a response, he was kissing her again as if his life depended on it. It was kind of cute, actually.

"A baby?" Alice pressed a hand against her still flat belly, hardly believing there was a baby nestled in there, the product of her and Kyvan's endless lovemaking. She had thought if she would fall pregnant, she would be devastated, but she was really kind of happy about it.

Alice wasn't too excited about the giving birth part, but she had to admit she couldn't wait until she had their baby in her arms. A product of her and Kyvan's love, even if their beginning had been less than perfect.

Kyvan saw her hesitation. "You are happy, aren't you, Alice?" He sucked in his breath. "Tell me what I can do to make you happy. I'll do anything—"

Alice interrupted him by using her hands to press against each of his cheeks to pull him forward. "You already make me very happy. I am glad about the baby, I promise. I was just surprised. I can't wait to meet our son."

Images of newborns, baby bottles, nurseries, and pacifiers started dancing her head. Yes, she was giving birth to a baby alien, but he would still be half human, meaning she would experience what normal mothers did before Kyvan started training him to be a warrior like he was.

Kyvan grinned like a happy puppy, pressing her against the examination bed. Alice was sure he would have made love to her right then and there, but Azis promptly kicked them out once he realized they were getting hot and heavy.

"How about we stop by the market?" he asked once they were back in the corridors. "We can get you a nice gift. Perhaps a new leash?"

Alice was about to respond to his teasing when they were nearly run over by a dozen warriors headed their way carrying spears, knives, and heavy chains. All of them were in their alien form, obviously prepared for some kind of battle. Alice's blood ran cold. Were they headed to another war?

Kyvan became serious at once as he gripped the arm of one of the aliens. "What has happened?"

"The king's pet has escaped," the other alien practically spat, his eyes narrowing with obvious disbelief. "Took one of our ships from right under our very noses. Even managed to turn off the tracking device. Made us look like complete fools to the king. Now we don't even know where the little brat has run off to. The king is furious."

"Why was I not informed?"

The alien shrugged, obviously annoyed at Kyvan's persistent questions. "I must go now. The king has threatened our manhood if we cannot find her before she blows her foolish head off or gets impregnated before the king has the opportunity to do it himself."

Before Kyvan could ask more questions, the other alien pulled away from him, following the herd. Alice and Kyvan stood quietly for a few seconds before he turned to look at Alice with a sharp look. "Alice, did you know about this? I won't whip your behind, not while you're pregnant, but I need to know. Did Karin mention anything about running away from the king?"

Alice nervously bit her pinky nail. "Maybe."

Kyvan gripped her shoulders. "Alice, you must tell me the truth. It is a dangerous universe out there. Planets are not always friendly to newcomers, especially humans. Karin could be killed or tortured for information. Is that what you want?"

"No," she blurted out before looking at her toes. "I don't know much, Kyvan, I swear. All she mentioned was that she was unhappy and she wanted to return to Earth. I didn't say anything because I never thought she would get away with it."

"Did she mention anything else? Those ships are hard to fly. It takes us weeks to learn." Kyvan bit his lip. "I'm surprised she even made it out of the platform."

Alice decided not to tell him they'd planned on running away together, to spare his feelings. "No."

Kyvan sighed as he hugged her tightly. "Thank you for telling me, little Alice. I shall let the king know."

Chapter 13

ALICE LOOKED at her flat belly in the mirror, viewing it from different angles, to see if there was any major differences since she had been told she was pregnant. She knew it was silly. She had just been told she was pregnant, so, of course, there wouldn't be any differences, but she could still try to see even a little something.

She had never thought pregnancy was something she would be excited for, she had thought it would be years before she got pregnant. But then again, her thinking had occurred when she had still been living on Earth and thought she would be focusing on a career and marriage before having a baby.

Her stubborn alien mate had gotten her pregnant in less than a year, and Alice couldn't help but think that everything had worked out exactly as it should.

Kyvan had told Alice they would stay at the palace for this baby, but as soon as their family grew, he would move them somewhere where he could still access the palace but where there was enough space for their kids to run around.

Alice wasn't too happy about the idea of her sons

becoming warriors and even less thrilled about being surrounded by all of the testosterone, but she had made peace with something she couldn't control. Besides, she knew Kyvan would keep them safe and make sure they would turn out to be fine and loyal warriors. Hell, he had managed to stay loyal to Korrev for many years even though the king was a complete ass.

Chicky was rubbing her body against her bare leg. She wasn't sure if she would still be comfortable walking around naked when she was more fully pregnant, but she did like being greeted by her mate's cock the second he walked in the door.

Alice had already warned him she would be wearing clothes fully outside of the bedroom the minute the babies came. Kyvan huffed but reluctantly agreed. What was it with aliens and them being comfortable with their own nudeness?

"What do you think, Chicky?" she asked her alien pet as she moved to the sides to check if she had gained even a small amount of weight. Nope, nothing. "Do you think I'll be a good mother?"

Chicky let out a sound between a yelp and a cry as she looked at Alice with loving eyes. At least she wouldn't be the only girl in the house. She then made her way upstairs to one of the guest bedrooms where she and Kyvan had decided the nursery would be.

She stood in the doorway. The room was empty now, but Kyvan had promised he would take her to the market as soon as he had time. He was still anxious about letting her out in public because of her newfound pregnancy status.

Alice was trying to be patient, but she felt her irritation growing. She hated being cooped up inside with nothing to do.

The girl flinched when she heard a knock on the door. Chicky started hissing immediately at the mere mention of an intruder. No wonder Kyvan had purchased her, she had no doubt Chicky would decapitate whoever was thinking of coming in if Alice let her.

"Calm down," she told her pet. Chicky narrowed her eyes at her as if silently calling her a fool.

Alice tried to hide her nervousness as she slipped a blue dress over her head, desperately wishing she had a weapon besides the knife she had managed to scoop up from the kitchen before she answered the door.

She had begged Kyvan to let her keep up with her training, but he had refused as soon as she turned out to be pregnant. Now she only had Chicky and this knife.

Alice wondered who it could be. No one ever visited their quarters, and while Kyvan was nice, no one could accuse him of being sociable. For a second, she thought about ignoring the knock, but what if it just made the person at the door angry?

She reluctantly opened the door, holding the knife with one hand while Chicky opened her mouth with anticipation, ready to ruin whoever came through the door.

The door swung open and Alice found herself stupidly closing her eyes, still holding the knife.

"What are you doing? Is that supposed to frighten me?"

Her blue eyes opened when she heard the bored tone associated it with. Chicky had dug her fangs on the king's leg in an attempt to bite it. Thankfully, Korrev was wearing a pair of thick, sturdy looking boots and Chicky did minimal damage with the exception of just making him extremely annoyed.

"Leave him, Chicky!" Alice picked up her pet after she put the knife down. Of course, Korrev wouldn't be frightened of her. It would be like a lion being frightened by a mouse. If he wanted to, the king could crush her throat, and she had a feeling the only reason he hadn't done so was because of his own loyalty to Kyvan. After all, she had been her present to him for being such a good warrior. "Sorry. I wasn't expecting guests."

She put down Chicky, who immediately went to go hide in the kitchen. So much for being protective. It wasn't the first time Korrev had visited their home, but he usually came to discuss personal matters with Kyvan, oftentimes ignoring her or making snide remarks about how she was below him.

This was the first time she had been alone with him since she walked in on Karin performing oral sex on him in the throne room.

Alice gulped. What could he possibly want? "Kyvan is not here."

"I know." He narrowed his eyes, looking at her as if she were a fool. "I came to talk to you?"

"Me?"

"Yes, you. Who else lives here besides you and Kyvan?"

Alice had always found the king scary and intimidating, but at the same time, majestic. He was almost too pretty to be a man, which was why she had thought he and Karin had made a beautiful couple the moment she had seen him. His long, golden hair and stunning ice-blue eyes would have gained him a modeling contract back home, but Alice knew he also craved violence. He loved war and fighting even more than Kyvan, and he could make his enemies scream in anguish in a matter of seconds. It was the reason why Alice tried not to be near him often. Korrev might like Kyvan, but he didn't like Alice.

Alice wondered how Karin had handled being his pet. Alice didn't think she could handle even five minutes with the guy.

However, she couldn't help but notice that, today, he looked less than majestic. He was paler than usual, with dark circles under his eyes. His blue eyes looked shifty instead of sharp, like they usually were, and for the first time, Alice saw an expression she had never seen before—fear.

The great King Korrev was actually frightened of something. She wondered what it was.

Alice reluctantly let him in. "Is it Kyvan? Is something wrong with him?" She knew the life of a warrior was dangerous. What if he left her widowed before the baby was even born?

King Korrev furrowed his brows. "Kyvan is fine. We're not at war, you know. Kyvan is stubborn, he will not die until he sees his son born."

Alice felt herself relax. She knew that, but it was nice to have it confirmed by someone else. "Is there anything I can do for you?"

The least she could do was be polite, and it was clear he was going through something.

"Yes." He turned around to face her until their bodies were practically placed together, her breasts rubbing against his chest. Alice felt herself blushing; she had never been so close to another man, even before she had been kidnapped. The only man in her life had been her alien mate.

Kyvan reached forward and pressed a hand around her neck, not tight enough to squeeze it, but uncomfortable enough to let her know he could break her neck if she pissed him off.

Alice stiffened. He had always been indifferent to her, but she had never thought he would be capable of threatening her. There wasn't even any point in screaming. Korrev was the king. If he so chose, he could execute her right then and there.

Alice felt the moisture gather around her eyes. She should have never opened the door. Now she found herself in this mess.

A hand went towards her belly, thinking of her unborn

child. Maybe Kyvan weas right and she was a walking magnet for danger. Her hands trembled as she gripped the king's wrist, which was easily the size of her neck.

She hated that she was trembling. She should have never put the knife down. For a second, she thought about calling out for Chicky, but Korrev looked crazy enough to harm her as well.

"Where is she?" he growled. His usual ice-blue eyes had darkened and his lips were pulled into a scowl.

Alice decided to play dumb even if it meant she was signing her own death sentence. "She?"

A growl escaped Korrev's lips and she was sure he was going to strangle her, but instead, he pulled back, removing his hand from her throat. He bent his knees slightly until they were looking at each other eye to eye.

For some reason, this felt more intimidating than having his hands around her throat.

"You know which 'she,'" Korrev stated, hitting the wall with his fists until they were a bloody mess. He then moved on to throwing whatever he could around him, smashing plates into pieces, throwing books across the room, and even tossing the furniture to the floor.

Alice had never seen him like this outside of battle. He was practically a monster. A monster hell bent on getting his pet back, even if he had to intimidate every soul who had ever so much as talked to her.

Korrev started to once again punch the wall like a mad man, blood pouring everywhere.

"Stop! Stop! You'll hurt yourself!" Alice finally cried out, not being able to take it. She had heard of people hurting themselves out of desperation, but she had never witnessed it.

Alice grabbed his wrist and forced him to stop using the wall like a punching bag.

"If you want me to stop, tell me where she is." The demand came coldly from his lips.

She swallowed. "I don't know, honest. I was healing after I got injured and we didn't spend much time together."

He nodded, taking in her explanation. At least the darkness had escaped from his eyes somewhat. Perhaps it had been a moment of insanity. "But she did mention her plans of running away?"

Alice nodded. It would come biting her back in the ass if she decided to lie at this moment. "Yes, but I didn't tell anyone, not even Kyvan, because I didn't think it was anything but a foolish dream. You have so many guards that, at the time, I thought it was impossible."

Korrev cocked his head, believing her. A humorless laugh escaped his lips. "Alice, I am a powerful king and a great warrior. Imagine being fooled by a little girl. I should be ashamed of myself, but I am highly impressed with Karin's abilities."

"Well, she was a lawyer before you kidnapped her. She's no dummy; if anyone could have found a way out, it would be Karin."

Korrev seemed to listen to her words carefully. "Why didn't I get a loyal mate like Kyvan, I wonder."

"Karin is not your mate; she's your pet."

"Pet. Mate. Both of those words just mean she belongs to me solely."

"Did you ever tell her that?"

He ignored her question. "So, you truly don't know where she ran off to? We can't even track down the ship's coordinates. She's managed to turn them off."

"I don't know where she went. All I know is she wanted to return to Earth."

"Her ship flew in the opposite direction before she managed to turn off the location. She wasn't going in the right direction." All traces of amusement left his face. "The outside worlds are dangerous. Karin could be getting killed or made prisoner at this moment. Alice, if you know anything else, now is the time to tell me."

"I don't." Alice couldn't believe she was actually starting to feel sorry for the coldhearted bastard. "I'm sorry."

The door opened fully, letting Kyvan in. He looked confused for a second about why the king and his mate were standing in the middle of a destroyed living room. Then he glared at Korrev, and before she could even blink, Kyvan had pressed Korrev against the opposite wall, nearly growling at him.

"What did you do? I told you Alice doesn't know anything about Karin. How dare you go into my private quarters and attack her!"

"Kyvan, he didn't attack me!" Alice cried, nearly crawling on top of him to pull him off the king. "I swear! He was just worried and frustrated about not being able to find Karin. I'm fine, trust me."

Kyvan hesitated as he looked between his mate and his king.

Korrev didn't look the least bit worried, even though one of his warriors looked like he wanted to crush his head. "It's true. I vented out my frustration on your belongings. For it, I apologize and I will make it up to you. Release me. Your mate will not suffer harm at my hands."

Kyvan let go of Korrev, the king straightened up and gave one curt nod to both of them before leaving.

Once he was out of their sight, Kyvan turned back to her, gripping her by her shoulders. "What happened? Are you hurt anywhere? Is the baby okay?"

"I'm fine, and the baby is fine," Alice reassured him and she watched Kyvan relax, a weary expression on his face. "He came to ask about Karin, and when I didn't have any new information, he vented out. He shouldn't have, but he didn't hurt me."

Kyvan let out a breath of relief. "I thought I was going to have to kill our king. He's been like a madman ever since Karin disappeared. He's losing his head trying to find the girl."

"Has he tried searching for her?" Alice rested her head against his chest, trying to get his beating heart to relax.

"Yes, he and other warriors have hardly stopped. I don't think the king has slept since she left. It's causing him to lose his composure. I've never seen him like this."

"Kyvan," she hesitated. "What if he doesn't find her? What if Karin is truly lost for good? What will happen to the king then?"

"He'll lose his mind without Karin."

Chapter 14

FOUR MONTHS LATER...

"I'm going to kill you!" Alice promised through gritted teeth four months after she had found out she was pregnant. She was seven months now and although she only had two more months to go, she felt swollen from her toes to her face and definitely very round.

On good days, she felt like a chubby squirrel and on bad days, she felt like a beach ball that definitely wanted to be deflated. She wiggled her toes, even though it had been at least a month since she had seen them. Alice had to make sure they were still there after all.

Despite her heavy pregnancy Alice was feeling quite content, something she never thought she would feel again when she had first been kidnapped. Each day, her baby was growing bigger and stronger as determined by the strong kicks he gave her belly when she didn't feed him properly or when his parents were a bit too rough in their lovemaking.

Though she was a little disappointed the gender wouldn't be a surprise since Kyvan pointed out all Krotev baby aliens were always born boys, never girls. Hell, her own child would more than likely follow in his father's footsteps and kidnap his own bride when he came of age.

Kyvan, who was terribly perceptive, noted her sadness about never having a baby girl despite trying to reassure him that gender disappointment was completely normal, nothing to make a fuss about. He still assured her he could get her an orphaned baby girl from Earth if she really wanted a daughter.

Alice assured him that, for now, she was content with just giving birth to their son, not to mention the half a dozen sons he would surely stuff her with. One baby and a strong, handsome husband was enough for the time being.

The brunette was just glad the fighting between planets had calmed down. Her baby needed a father, and she needed a husband.

Kyvan looked at her wearily from where he was making dinner. He had been an absolute prince ever since he had found out she was pregnant, cooking her dinner, massaging her swelling feet, and dealing with her whiny attitude.

Best of all, Alice hadn't been spanked since she had found out she was pregnant, which had made her act extra bratty since she knew Kyvan didn't have the heart to punish her.

"What is it now, brat?" He pressed a piece of soft bread against her lips and she swallowed.

"I'm too big," she whined, but she accepted another piece of bread. "It's all your fault. You keep feeding me."

"Because I want you and our baby to be strong." Kyvan kissed her forehead. "Besides, when you mate with us, it's expected you will have big babies."

Alice grumbled about payback as she rubbed her big belly. His little feet gave pleasurable little kicks and she smiled. She could hardly wait for their baby to be in her arms.

Kyvan lay down on the couch next to her. He then wrapped his arms around her so he was the big spoon, cradling her large belly in his hand.

Alice started stroking his arms, enjoying the warm feeling of his body against hers. She couldn't explain the large amount of love she felt towards Kyvan. It sometimes felt so huge, it was almost like her heart was going to explode out of her chest.

It still surprised her the way her feelings had changed towards Kyvan. She had gone from despising the man because he had kidnapped her to not wanting to be away from him for too long, especially as she approached the due date.

"I know you don't like being pregnant, but you look beautiful, my love." Kyvan started peppering her with kisses as she snuggled closer to him.

"Really? I don't look like a whale?"

"I do not know what a whale is, but no. Or if you do, you are the prettiest of whales."

"You are just saying that because you want me pregnant again."

"Could you blame me? It's in my blood. I want to constantly fill you with my child."

She laughed. "You're a terrible beast."

They had recently discussed moving out of the palace and into their own large home with an actual garden, so their children could run around. Alice would be glad of it, especially if she didn't have to worry about Korrev roaming around.

Though, to be fair, she hadn't seen much of the king ever since Karin managed to escape and remove the tracker. She only knew from Kyvan that the king was still searching for her day in and day out, using his most advanced spaceships and his best men, but still no word from her.

Her old apartment had even been searched, but it seemed she had not returned. Alice didn't know if she should be glad or worried they still hadn't found Karin. She didn't know much about other planets, but from the bits and pieces she had heard, Krotev was almost tame in comparison.

Alice and Kyvan were just starting to fall asleep when there was a loud knock on the door. Kyvan sighed as he removed Alice from his body and went to answer the door. Through the corner of her eye, she saw a gray alien, with the red eyes that scared her so much, talking to Kyvan. She recognized the bushy red hair; he had been one of the men she had seen when she had first woken up on this godforsaken planet.

He was frowning, and Alice remembered him frowning on the day she woke up as well. He and Kyvan were speaking in low voices. No matter how much she wanted to overhear, she couldn't.

After what seemed like forever, Kyvan nodded, then closed the door behind the alien. He looked surprised when he saw her wobbling towards him with a hand on her lower back to keep herself steady.

"What did he want?" she demanded.

Her mate raised an eyebrow. "And how is it any of your business, troublemaker?" She glared at him and he sighed. "Korrev found Karin."

Alice's eyes widened in disbelief as she placed a hand on her large belly. Karin had disappeared shortly after Alice found out she was pregnant and had decided to stay at her mate's side. She had to give her points for having the balls to steal a plane from under King Korrev's nose.

A part of her wanted to applaud Karin for being able to go into hiding for four months even with the king hunting her down himself, but another part of her was worried over Karin's safety. She was a human female, after all, which, on some planets, was basically asking to be a target.

Sometimes when she was feeling pessimistic, Alice wondered if Karin was dead. Apparently, the blonde had nine lives. She felt a sharp pain in her lower belly, reminding her she was giving birth in two months, something she was not looking forward to even though Kyvan assured her she would be knocked out as soon as she started feeling labor pains. Krotev's advanced medicine really came in handy.

Kyvan noticed Alice wincing and immediately scooped her up in his arms bridal style, as if she weighed no more than three pounds. Well, he had been working out more. Alice had teased him once or twice if he really thought he could protect them on pure muscle alone, something Kyvan had definitely not found amusing.

"Bed. Now." He frowned. "I told you, you need to be taking it easy. Why are you being so naughty today? Do you need a spanking?

"No," she whined. The only spanking she had received since she had found out she was pregnant was the occasional love tap, but it was only when she was getting on Kyvan's last nerve. "You promised no more spankings until the baby is born."

He kissed her temple in warning as he placed her on the bed. "Then behave."

Alice started squirming around on the bed. "Can I go see her? How is she doing? Is Korrev pissed? How did they find her? I know you mentioned I should call him King Korrev, but it sounds a little uppity, don't you think?"

"Enough," Kyvan interrupted, obviously annoyed at all

her questions. "You cannot see Karin, Alice. Now, why don't you lie in bed and I'll bring you Chicky so she can keep you company."

"Why can't I see her?" Alice demanded, gripping his arm. "Is Korrev going to punish her?"

Kyvan sighed, obviously wanting to have another conversation. "That is none of our business. If Karin didn't want to be punished, then she shouldn't have run away. Korrev is her master; she is his pet. She was expected to stay, but she disobeyed. He has every right to punish her."

She raised an eyebrow, trying not to show her disgust. "Would you have punished me if I had run away?" She doubted she would have been able to get away with it, Karin was more clever than she was.

"What do you think?"

Alice sighed as she rested her body against the pillows. "I just hope he isn't cruel to her, he has a mean grip." Her blue eyes widened in horror. "You don't think he'll kill her, right? Maybe do a public execution, to warn everyone?"

Kyvan stared at her, before he burst out laughing.

Alice scowled as she whacked him on the shoulder. "It's not funny!"

"It is when you say absurd stuff like that." He started running a hand through her silky black locks which had grown longer throughout her pregnancy. "Do you really think the king would kill her after he spent all his energy and time looking for her?"

"I guess not."

Kyvan lay down next to her, pulling her close as she rested in his arms. They were silent for a few minutes until she spoke again. "May I pretty please visit her once Korrev finishes punishing her? Come on, he can't ground her forever. I want to see her before the baby comes."

Kyvan hesitated.

"What? Is something wrong?"

"Alice, Karin's return wasn't as smooth as we had hoped. Korrev's messenger informed me that Karin is very sick. She ate something from the planet they picked her up from which, apparently, does not dwell well in a human's immune system. She's with Azis right now, but it's not looking too good. She's delirious with fever, so we don't know exactly how much she ate."

Alice felt herself grow cold at the thought of losing her friend. Brave, beautiful, intelligent Karin. "Is she going to die?"

"Do you really believe Korrev will allow her to die before he properly thrashes her behind for running away?" He squeezed her tightly. "Don't worry, troublemaker, I'm sure Karin will be fine. She always is."

"When can I visit her?"

"When she gets better," he stressed as he poked her belly. "Or when our son is finally born."

Alice pouted.

Kyvan changed the subject. "Are you excited about meeting our baby? You've been a tad restless lately."

"You noticed?"

"I notice everything about you, little Alice."

Alice smiled at him, pleased. "The answer is yes. He's been moving inside me so much, I can't wait to finally have him in my arms." She gave him a warning look. "But don't even think about getting me pregnant again as soon as this baby is born. I'm serious, Kyvan."

"We'll see."

"Kyvan! I mean it, I'm not a baby-making machine. Where are we going to put them all?"

"I'll build you a larger house."

"Kyvan—"

He interrupted her by landing a kiss on her lips. She

glared at him. "You just want me to shut up."

A smirk curled on his lips, but he didn't deny or agree to the statement. "I love you, my little mate."

Alice raised her head. "Forever?"

"Forever."

Epilogue

"HOW ARE YOU FEELING?"

"How do I look?"

Alice smiled at Karin's idea of a joke, but the smile quickly disappeared from her face when the blonde erupted into loud coughs. She reached forward and plucked one of the heavily decorated handkerchiefs from the nightstand next to her. Of course, Korrev would think simple tissues or, at the very least, rags were beneath him and essentially the person he viewed as an extension of himself.

His obsession with Karin would have been cute if he didn't insist on being a controlling asshole. But then again, Karin had managed to successfully outrun him for months, something not even his finest warriors had managed to do, so it wasn't odd he was feeling a bit wary about letting her out of his sight.

The only reason Alice had been allowed to visit, was because Korrev was worried about Karin feeling lonely and her not getting any better even after months of treatment. Kyvan hadn't been thrilled about letting her visit, either.

After all, she was about to give birth any moment now and should be in the maternity ward.

"You look perfect. Like you."

Karin rolled her eyes as she took a dainty sip of water. "You're just like Korrev, a terrible liar. Both of you are too blunt to be dishonest. I know I look horrendous."

Horrendous was probably a harsh word, but Alice was sure the beauty she had come to know was still there somewhere. Once the illness cleared up, Karin would be back to her old self, but she had heard the poison she had accidentally drunk was fatal to humans and she had managed to scrape by, by the skin of her teeth. It was the reason why the palace healers were overworked and she hadn't been able to leave the palace in two months.

Karin's skin was paler than it usually was, resembling the color of the moon, but less beautiful. There were dark circles under her eyes which made her look like she had been punched in the face. Alice could see how skinny she'd gotten; her arms looked almost breakable, and she could see her collarbone protruding from the paper-thin skin. Her once golden hair was so thin, it was almost falling out.

She looked like a walking corpse, not that Alice would ever tell her. Before she had gone in, Korrev had practically hissed into her ear that he wanted positive words only. Alice had bitten her tongue in order not to snap at him.

"It will be over soon," Alice tried to reassure her brightly. "You'll feel better before you know it and then we can resume our playdates, except I'll have a baby in tow."

Karin closed her eyes. "I don't think I'll ever get better. It's been two months since I was rescued and I still feel so tired. All I want to do is sleep, and I can barely digest a meal."

"Do the healers know what it is?"

"They said the poison is out of my system, my body is

just recuperating, but since I'm human, it takes longer. They're giving me all these tonics and pills, but to be honest, I don't think it's doing much."

No wonder Korrev was out of his mind. Kyvan had mentioned the king had been more short-tempered and distracted recently, but Alice hadn't thought Karin had been the reason. After all, he had the whole palace to wait on her.

Apparently, he was more concerned about the little blonde than he let on.

"I miss the sun," Karin blurted out, breaking the silence. "And the beach. And hot dogs. I regret not going to the beach more when I was in New York. I think I just assumed it would always be there."

Krotev wasn't chilly, but it definitely didn't get as hot here as it did on Earth. Kyvan had pointed out it was because their species tended to run hot, which was the result of cooler weather. At least, it wasn't snowing. Alice would describe the weather as an average seventy degrees.

Alice closed her eyes. "And ice cream and a bonfire with chocolate and smores."

"Chocolate. I would give my left arm if I could have a chocolate bar."

"I'm sure Korrev would be more than happy to send for one if it meant you would eat."

Silence.

The topic of Korrev seemed to render her speechless. Alice had thought Karin was afraid of the king, but lately, it seemed she was unsure of her standing. Before she escaped, she had been nothing more than a pet whose only role was to please the king or risk a hot bottom. Now, she was being treated like a delicate little thing and fussed over constantly, with the king agreeing to everything she asked of him. No wonder the poor girl was confused.

"Let's leave him out of this," she finally murmured.

Karin's blue eyes settled on Alice's large, protruding belly. It was seven days before her due date and Alice was feeling ginormous and every part of her body felt swollen. "Are you sure you're not carrying twins? No offense, but you look like you're an overindulged cat."

"Thanks for the compliment," she murmured sarcastically. "That doesn't terrify me at all."

Karin winced. "Sorry, I've never given birth. I'm sure everything will be fine."

Kyvan had admitted giving birth on his planet was more advanced than back on Earth, almost a completely painless experience which is why so many human mates gave birth often. Alice took his word with a grain of salt. He was a warrior, after all, and he didn't know much about giving birth and recuperating afterwards.

"Have you thought about names?"

"Not really, Kyvan wants to name him after his father, but it's quite a mouthful. I don't think I want to give such a difficult name to a baby. Since I knew it was going to be a boy, I thought it was going to be easier, but no such luck. Do you think you would ever want to have a baby?"

Karin shrugged. "Mates have babies. Pets don't."

"But you don't know if you're a pet anymore."

"Bad pets who run away don't get rewarded. That's what the king said," Karin said flatly. "He will never raise my status to anything but a pet. Why do you think I tried running away? Do you really think he would let a little troublemaker like me give birth to his princes?"

Alice didn't say anything, but she couldn't help but feel that Korrev had changed. He had definitely grown softer in the past few months. Not to mention, sooner or later, he would need to sire some heirs.

"The question is do you want to give birth to his princes?"

Karin opened her mouth to argue with her, but Korrev chose at that moment to slip into the room, not caring he was interrupting. He barely looked in Alice's direction even though he had been the one to beg her to come.

"Alice, leave, now."

Alice scowled at him, but she relaxed when she saw Karin nod in her direction. At least, Korrev wasn't being an asshole in private. The bastard was actually kneeling down next to the blonde as he squeezed her hand.

"How are you feeling?"

"Much better, my king, thank you," Karin murmured. She looked up at Alice. "Visiting with Alice did me good. You should come back again when you can, Alice, and bring your baby with you. I would love to meet him."

Alice nodded before glaring at Korrev. She didn't care if Kyvan spanked her for her outburst, someone needed to give him a piece of mind. "You'd better treat her with respect, or I will make you very sorry—"

"Of course, I have nothing but respect for my queen," King Korrev interrupted with a slight smirk to his lips.

Both women stared at him.

Karin's eyes widened in a mixture of disbelief and fascination. "Your queen?"

He pecked her lips. "Yes, my queen. Once you are well, we will make it official and we will work on siring princes. How does that sound?"

Karin looked lost for once. She gulped. "That would be acceptable."

"Good." He looked pleased before he turned back to Alice. "I believe I dismissed you, Alice."

Alice nodded, resting her hand on her belly as Karin and Korrev kept looking at each other with such an adoring gaze. To think they had been at each other's throats months ago.

Leaving the lovebirds alone, she made her way outside

where Kyvan was waiting patiently for her. She would never get tired of this, having her mate wait for her and being adored by him.

Yes, she wasn't pleased when he chose to discipline her, but she knew he did it out of love and he always made it up to her later.

"How was Karin?"

He pressed a hand on her lower back as they started walking back to their quarters. "Better," Alice admitted. "She still looks a bit weak, but she lit up when she saw Korrev. I think she fancies him even if she won't admit it."

"Love can often be more powerful than hate," Kyvan said wisely. "And the king does care about Karin in his own way. He nearly lost his mind when he was looking for her."

"He's going to make her his queen."

Kyvan looked stunned. "How do you know?"

"He just told her. Apparently, I am going to be friends with the queen."

"I don't think much will change." He looked amused. "But I'm glad you're happy. I don't remember the last time our planet had a queen. Perhaps Queen Karin will be the first."

Alice was about to respond when she felt a sharp pain underneath her belly. Their son often kicked and moved, demanding her attention, but it had never been this painful. Alice bit her lip when she felt another sharp pain. She hoped they had the good drugs, otherwise, she didn't think she was going to make it without screaming the palace down.

A yelp escaped her when she felt like her entire lower section was being ripped open by claws.

Kyvan placed his hands around her hips to steady her, worry spreading across his face. "What is it? What's wrong? Is the baby coming?"

Alice was about to reassure him that everything was fine.

For someone who was a fierce warrior, the idea of a baby really sent him into a panic. "Alice, talk to me, is it the baby?"

The pressure in her lower regions was growing and she was afraid she was going to give birth in this hallway. Why did half alien babies have to be so damn big? If she tore any part of herself, Alice was going to make sure Kyvan and Korrev got her a nice present. She was adding to the population of their planet after all.

Before she could respond, she felt something slipping down her legs and onto her bare feet. Her water had broken and the pain was quickly becoming worse. She knew human babies often took hours to make an appearance, but she wasn't sure about alien babies and she wasn't going to run the risk of giving birth without a healer there.

"Yes," she managed to huff between contractions. "The baby is coming. Now."

"Okay, all right. Nothing to worry about," Kyvan stuttered as he picked her up in his arms. "We will be all right, I swear to you, Alice. I'll get you to a healer soon, and then—"

"Relax," Alice interrupted him by kissing him sweetly. "I can do this. You get me to the healers. I'll be fine, I know what to do."

Kyvan nodded as he kissed her forehead. "We're going to meet our baby soon, little Alice."

"Our little boy." Alice wrapped her arms around his neck, smiling at him.

"I'll protect you both," Kyvan swore, hugging her protectively to his chest. "My family."

Annabelle Marin

Annabelle Marin is a twenty-something romantic who lives in sunny California. When she isn't writing she enjoys daydreaming, watching way too much TV, and cuddling with her pets.

Her books are sweet erotic romances with domestic discipline. In her books you can expect: a spoonful of sweetness, a dash of sass, a cup of naughtiness, and an abundance of romance.

You can follow Annabelle on Facebook, Instagram, Goodreads, and Bookbub for exciting updates on upcoming books!

Facebook-https://www.facebook.com/annabelle.marin.940/
Instagram-https://www.instagram.com/
missannabellemarin/
Bookbub-//www.bookbub.com/profile/annabelle-marin
Goodreads-www.goodreads.com/author/show/21061973.
Annabelle_Marin

Don't miss these exciting titles by Annabelle Marin and Blushing Books!

Endless Paradise
Between Kisses & Lies
Letters to Holly
On the Dotted Line
His Southern Belle

Earthly Mates
The Alien's Mate

The Benningtons
Holy Matrimony

The Hollis Sisters
The Affair
The Scandal

The Stevenson Brothers Series
The Rancher Orders a Bride
The Pastor Takes a Wife
The Sheriff Finds a Fiancée

Vintage Beauties Series
Bless Her Heart
Becoming a Gibson Girl
The Modern Housewife

The Bride Series
The Unwilling Mrs.
The Unattainable Bride
The Unexpected Wife

Anthologies
12 Naughty Days of Christmas 2021

Blushing Books

Blushing Books Newsletter

Please join the Blushing Books newsletter
to receive updates & special promotional offers.
You can also join by using your mobile phone:
Just text BLUSHING to 22828.

www.ingramcontent.com/pod-product-compliance
Lightning Source LLC
Chambersburg PA
CBHW020342260626
47156CB00004B/1653